Anna Mae Mysteries
The Golden Treasure

L. S. Cauldwell

SP

a Star Publish Book
www.starpublishllc.com

ISBN: (Paperback) 1-932993-98-3
ISBN 13: 978-1932993-98-1

Library of Congress Number
LCCN: 2008938603

Edited by Star Publish
Cover Design by Ben Caldwell
Interior Design by Alicia McMullen

Published in 2008 by Star Publish LLC
www.starpublishllc.com
Printed in the United States of America

Anna Mae Mysteries
The Golden Treasure

Acknowledgements

I want to thank Dr. Barry Jacobson, Rowena Cherry, Jacqueline Lichtenberg, Karen MacLeod, and Janet Elaine Smith for editing *The Anna Mae Mysteries: The Golden Treasure.*

I want to thank Marlive Harris of The Grits Agency and Grits Kids Book Club members and their parents for their help, advice and suggestions in improving the vernacular and lexicon of Granma Zora Kingsley, Anna Mae and Malcolm Botts.

I want to thank Mary Welk, mystery author, for reading *The Anna Mae Mysteries* and informing me that I had a good plot and storyline.

I want to thank Trish Shields and her twelve-year-old daughter Candice, and Geoff Nelder for reviewing *The Anna Mae Mysteries* before its release.

I want to thank Lewis Anderson, retired firefighter, for helping me with the fire scenes at Anna Mae Botts' school. Without his help, I would have never gotten the scenes right. Thank you, Lewis!

I want to thank Alana Burke for telling me where Chennault Plantation was located in Lincoln, Georgia, 2005.

Map of Northeast Georgia and Jefferson Davis's Flight in May 1865

to ATLANTA

Abbeville, SC

SOUTH CAROLINA

Chennault Plantation

Washington

Lowery

Lincolnton

Augusta

Savannah River

to SAVANNAH

Warthen

Sandersville

Dublin

Ocmulgee River

Oconee River

Gum Swamp River

GEORGIA

Abbeville, GA

Jefferson Davis Surrenders Here

Irwinville

AnnaMarie's
Treasure Search Route

Jefferson Davis's
Flight Through Georgia

PROLOGUE

At the beginning of the Civil War, Jefferson Davis, President of the Confederate States, took out a loan from a French Banking House of Emile Erlanger for $15 million dollars. The face value of the loan was more like $8.5 million at that time.

The House stipulated that Jefferson Davis must pay back the loan in ten years, with interest, whether he won or lost the war.

"In 1865, the night of May 24, two wagon trains, filled with gold—one containing the loan money from France and the other money from Virginia banks— were robbed at Chennault Crossroads in Lincoln County.

"Chennault Plantation, owned by Dionysius Chennault, an elderly planter and Methodist minister, was to help return the gold to France. Jefferson Davis gave his word that the gold would be returned.

"The guarded wagons made it as far as Augusta before they were waylaid by Union troops. One wagon escaped and made its way back to Chennault Plantation.

"The jubilation didn't last long. About 100 yards from the porch of the plantation house, the gold disappeared!

One theory was that the French gold was buried at the confluence of the Apalachee and Oconee rivers. Some say that it was divided up among the locals while others smile and turn away content to keep their secret and take it to their graves.

"Legend persists that the treasure was hastily buried on the original grounds of Chennault Plantation and remains there to this day."

Chapter One

Thunder rumbled in the distance. Heat lightening crackled in the swirling sky above, jolting my already raw nerves. I wanted to jump up into the air, but my feet refused to move. Raul Garcia, my best friend from sixth grade, dragged me forward into the schoolyard. My eight-year-old brother Malcolm trudged beside me. None of us wanted school to start yet, summer had seemed far too short. I noticed that Raul's normal smile drooped a bit too.

"It won't be so bad this year," Raul said. "I won't let Pit Bull hurt you. You'll see. I'm stronger and bigger."

"Yeah, right," I said.

I peered down at my new pink sneakers with red shoelaces. Dust and dirt clung to the white rubber edges. I loitered in the yard, wishing school was over and we were on our way home. A thin, whistling wind blew across my cheeks, cooling them from the last oppressive heat of summer.

"Anna Mae, look out!"

Malcolm's trembling voice broke through my daydreaming. He shoved some old, gnarled and rotten thing under my nose. My eyes watered. I sneezed and looked down.

"Yuk! What is it?"

Raul pushed his stolid body between us. He picked up the offensive object from Malcolm's palm and held it up in front of his eyes.

"It's...a...ginger...root!"

The breeze whipped through the schoolyard. Swings swung forward and crashed backwards, their chains interlocking. Loose papers skimmed the ground. The tin garbage can fell to the ground, banging against the packed dirt and loose stones. Two raindrops fell and bounced off my nose. I looked up and gasped.

Floating in mid air a large black, disembodied manacled fist blocked our path. It appeared from out of nowhere. Malcolm ducked and hid behind me.

"I don't believe it's really there," Raul said

He stepped in front of me and raised his own puny fists. The root fell from his hands. The black fist hovered in sight, but out of reach. I know, because Raul jumped into the air, swinging at it.

"Anna Mae..."

Malcolm's voice ripped through my mind. I inched backwards and grabbed his arm.

"Look!"

I followed his pointing finger. The root crept forward; its tendrils waving. It reminded me of the sacred roots that Granma Zora used in her mojos. The root mimicked the movements of its counterpart overhead. What I wanted to know was where the rest of its body was.

Saliva soured in my mouth. I shivered. The wind moaned. I almost howled along with it. I noticed that the blades of grass lay flat as if a heavy foot crushed them into the dirt. Around us, nothing else stirred. The thingy overhead stood still. Its chain rattled. Goosebumps raced up my arms. My teeth chattered. By my side, Malcolm whined. He was no longer my brother/knight in shining armor.

"Granma, I know you're here. Granma?" he said.

I stamped both feet on the ground.

"She ain't here! She's home at St. Simons. 'Member the mojo she sent me?

Poppa was madder than hell. He hates magik. That's why she nevah comes and visits us any more. 'Member what Momma said? Nevah agin will she cross our door. Nevah!"

I jerked forwards. Something whomped me from the rear. I stumbled. Raul tried catching me. Fifteen yards separated us from the main school building.

Malcolm ducked and cringed. The black fist disappeared, then reappeared above our heads. I didn't cower. I bit my lip and stood on my tiptoes, studying it. I noticed a gold wedding band on its fourth finger. The slender fingers were clean, although the skin was cracked and wrinkled. My toes gave out. I fell backwards. Malcolm cushioned my fall as we both crumpled to the dirt. Raul turned back and helped me to my feet.

The fist paralleled our movements, staying close, but out of reach. Malcolm pinched my arm. "I've gotta go, Anna Mae. It's killing me!"

"Cross your legs!" Raul hissed.

"Hush, both of you."

The first bell rang. I looked at my watch. It was five minutes past eight. We had to hurry or we'd be late. Malcolm whimpered behind me. Raul moved closer, his breathing controlled.

"I don't like it."

I stared at the clenched hand. It hung in mid-air. I saw no strings or wires. It just appeared.

"Is it solid?"

"I...I guess so. I can't see nothin' on the othahh side."

Malcolm clutched his stomach and bent over. "I can't hold it in."

"Then go!" I shouted, not caring about him.

The floating object held my attention. Nothing could distract me except for that accursed ginger root. It was now resting about ten feet away from Malcolm.

"I'm gone!" Malcolm whispered, and fled.

I heard him, yet it seemed like I didn't. Malcolm's voice meant nothing as long as that thingy stayed in front of me. Raul put his arm around my waist and squeezed me. I felt the warmth from his arm.

"Hadn't we better leave too?"

"You go. That fist..."

Raul turned to go. The fist's fingers unfolded. Two paper scraps fluttered out and fell in dizzying circles. I watched the scraps as they floated and spun. I saw Raul grab one piece before it hit the ground. He brought it up close to his glasses and read it aloud. "Find the gold!"

"That doesn't make any sense."

I stooped over and picked up the second paper from the ground. I read it. "Find the house where Davis lost it."

"This either. Gold, house, Davis, lost...it's strange."

We stopped talking. The hand re-clenched and moved closer to us, as if it was trying to listen. Was it reading our lips? Raul ignored it. He turned and faced me, cupping my cheeks with his hands so my eyes focused on his.

"I better go find Malcolm and make sure he made it all right. I'll meet you at the classroom door before the next bell rings."

I nodded and watched the weird object. It didn't move when Malcolm dashed off; it just kept hovering in front of me. I took that as a good sign. I took one giant step forward. The black fist moved with me and changed directions when I did. It blocked my path. I couldn't leave.

At my feet, I felt the ginger root attack me. I glanced down. The root's tendrils twisted and looped through my shoelaces. Tied together, I couldn't take a step in any direction. The thingy above and the root below caught a trespasser—me.

A spitball struck the back of my neck. I twisted, forgetting the black fist and the ginger root. Behind me, Stanley Paxton stood. I called him "The Pit Bull of the Playground." He wore a new green and white football jersey with the number twelve printed on it. His black jeans sagged around his hips. His pants' cuffs dragged in the dirt and rode over boots that were almost as spit-n-polished as my father's shoes were.

"What happened to your boyfriend?"

"Don't know what you mean."

I kept my tone even. One didn't dare show fear to Stanley. Compared to the fist and the ginger root, he posed a greater threat to me. I waited for his next move.

"How come you're not in class?"

"Not sure I wanna go."

The second bell rang. I scratched my nose.

"You're gonna be late."

"Just as late as you gonna be."

I wasn't going to tell him that two *thingies* prevented me from going inside. Stanley didn't believe in ghosts, werewolves or vampires. A UFO and a ginger root appearing in the schoolyard wouldn't bother him. He wouldn't understand it, and he wouldn't see them either. Neither one existed in his mind's eye. Dropping paper clues from out of nowhere and waving tendrils knotting shoelaces were beyond his brainpower.

"Gotta go."

I lifted my left foot. Nothing happened. I turned my head and tilted it. The disembodied hand was gone.

I heard a deep guttural laughter. I twisted my head and gaped. It now blocked Pit Bull's path. He tried dodging it, but the fist appeared to grow in size until it dwarfed Stanley. I shook my head, blinked my eyes, and rubbed them hard. I even put on my reading glasses. Nothing did the trick. A gigantic object overshadowed Pit Bull. At his feet, the ginger root rocked on two of its thick trunks.

He cringed, blubbering in their presence. "Don't hurt me."

The fist reshaped its fingers. I saw it give me the thumbs-up sign. Pit Bull had buried his face in the dirt and lay still. I gasped and tried to collect my thoughts. Raul appeared out of nowhere and grabbed me by the arm.

"What are you waiting for? The third bell is about to ring. We've gotta go. Malcolm made it to the john. He bumped into his teacher, Mr. Santos, in the hallway. Don't worry about him. We'll be in trouble, not Malcolm."

We ran towards the school building. A hall monitor had propped one of the doors open with a chair. I saw Ms. Yolanda, our seventh grade homeroom teacher, by the door, with her clipboard and pen in her hand. I knew what that meant. Raul and I didn't have enough time to make it to our lockers.

I stumbled on the curb. Raul dragged me in. Ms. Yolanda stared at her pocket watch, counting the seconds.

"You made it. Better get to homeroom. You can find your lockers later."

Chapter Two

I shuddered as we tramped through the hallway. Bleak, green water-stained walls greeted us as if we were old friends. Warped metal locker doors creaked on rusty hinges as they popped opened. The mismatched green-tinted cracked floor tiles held firm beneath our sneakered feet. Water dripped down the concrete walls. The building smelled like a garbage dump: an obnoxious blend of stale cigarette smoke, marijuana and unwashed bodies.

Breathing through parted lips, I tried not to inhale the foul sulfur blend. Raul clapped his hands over his mouth. He snorted. It sounded like a cross between a dry cough and a gag.

The stench followed us down the hall to Ms. Yolanda's homeroom, our sanctuary for the next nine months. Raul reached out and opened the classroom door. It moaned as it opened. I trudged into the room, clutching my chest. Twenty-eight eyes rose from their desks and inspected me. The black kids pointed and giggled. The Hispanics and Asians looked up, stared, and then dropped their eyes. The white kids looked right through me, as if I was an invisible person not worth their notice.

I saw that the classroom was set up no differently than it had been when I was in sixth grade. The white kids, or the "adventurers" as they preferred to be called, sat on the right side of the room closest to the door, blackboard, and teacher. The second-class whites, those the adventurers called "charity settlers," sat on the left side of the room. The middle and back part of the room was where the Hispanics and the Asian kids sat. None of them talked amongst themselves either.

Christine Harper, a sixth grade friend from last year, waved at me. She pointed towards a group of empty desk-chairs. There were four of them, grouped together in a circle and set apart. I stepped towards the desk-chair facing forwards. Removing my backpack, I shoved it between the bottom rungs of the chair. Straightening, I sat down, fanning my hot face with my right hand. It helped somewhat.

Lola Simms, Pit Bull's girlfriend from last year, raised her middle finger and aimed it at me. She sat in the second row in the fourth desk. Her green and white football shirt hugged her chest and matched Pit Bull's. She smiled—a tiger shark smile. I dropped my eyes and focused on the scarred desk's wooden surface. My fingertips traced the individual carved letters on top: S-H-I...! It didn't help. The rest of Pit Bull's gang—Michael Jakobs, John Fry, Mark Somers, Stuart Langston, Herman Potts, and Joey Fritz—sat around their enthroned queen and threw spitballs at me. Mutual loathing crackled between us.

Raul chose the desk-chair facing the windows. He thrust his backpack under the chair and sat down without looking around. Behind me, Christine sighed, leaned forward, and leered at him.

"Hi, Raul. Have a nice summer?"

Raul ignored her and focused his eyes on Ms. Yolanda as she entered the classroom. The final bell rang at eight fifteen. She carried the clipboard and pocket watch in her left hand. She strolled to her desk and placed them on top of it. Without saying a word, Ms. Yolanda marched up to the board and taped a large portrait picture in the far left corner of the board. She saluted the picture, and then turned, facing us. I squinted at the board. President Clinton beamed back at me.

"Good morning, class," Ms. Yolanda said, first in English and then in Spanish. "Buenos dias, clase."

The class answered back in both Spanish and English.

"Buenos dias, Señorita Yolanda." "Good morning, Ms. Yolanda."

Lola Simms raised her hand first. I held my breath. Ms. Yolanda glanced at her. "Do you have a question?"

"Yes, Ms. Yolanda. I do."

"And you are?"

"Lola Simms. What kind of perfume are you wearing?"

The class burst into nervous laughter. Behind me, I heard Catherine mutter, "I wish I'd thought of that first, but you know Lola."

"Everyone knows Lola," I whispered back.

Ms. Yolanda frowned.

"See me after school. Now, class, while I take roll call, if you'll take out your notebooks, I want you to write a one-page report about what extraordinary event happened to you this summer. Raise your hand when you hear your name. After I finish, each of you will stand by your desk and read your paper aloud."

A collective groan rumbled through the room. Ms. Yolanda ignored it. She sat down and opened her black rollback. I watched as she thumbed to the first page. Ms. Yolanda picked up the 12-inch ruler that lay on her desk. Placing it underneath the first name, she called it out, starting with the last name that began with the letter "A."

"Roberto Arnolds."

Robert raised his hand and dropped it. He chewed on his pen, but kept his eyes glued to his notebook paper.

"Wendy Banks."

I didn't know Wendy. She looked Asian, with her slanted eyes and high cheekbones. Wendy reminded me of the teen cashier down at the corner fast-food grocery store. Like the cashier, Wendy said nothing and shot her hand up and down before Ms. Yolanda noticed it. I wondered if Wendy wanted to disappear into the woodwork like I did from time to time.

"Wendy Banks!" Ms. Yolanda caught sight of Wendy's hand the second time. My name was called next.

"Anna Mae Botts."

I raised my hand, then dropped it into my lap. Lola Simms popped her chewing gum with a long red fingernail. She chewed and passed it from cheek to cheek, as if to get more mileage from it. Chewing gum was a "not permitted rule" in sixth grade. I wondered if Lola would have to spit it out.

Ms. Yolanda stared in Lola's direction, but seemed reluctant to start an all-out war just yet. I sighed and picked up my pen. Staring at the blue-lined white paper, the spaces merged together. My kid brother popped into my head. I wrote down our scooter adventure. I didn't hear Ms. Yolanda calling out any other names until I heard Pit Bull's name called.

"Stanley Paxton."

No answer. She repeated his name. "Stanley Paxton?"

Again, no one answered. The class drew in a collective breath. Ms. Yolanda stared at a desk in front of Lola Simms. Manuel Martinez sat up straight.

"You're sitting in the wrong seat," Ms. Yolanda said, clearing her throat.

"Yeah, well, I thought it was okay, seeing it was a new school year."

Ms. Yolanda tried not to glare at him.

"There are unspoken rules one doesn't break, not even in the new school year. Please sit with Raul Garcia and Anna Mae Botts. There are two empty desk-chairs there."

Manuel rose from the chair. He picked up his notebook and sauntered to the front of the class. He smirked as he trod past Ms. Yolanda's desk and walked towards Raul and me. Selecting the desk-chair opposite Raul, he sat down, facing the door, Lola Simms, and Pit Bull's gang of five. Ms. Yolanda sniffed, and then addressed the rest of the class.

"Anyone know where Stanley Paxton is this morning?"

My face burned. I stared at Raul's chest. I felt his hand squeeze my shoulder. I peered up. My nose quivered. I stopped breathing and opened my mouth. Ms. Yolanda's perfume spread up my nostrils, and I gagged. I was allergic to perfume and forgot all about that Ms. Yolanda loved wearing flower fragrances.

Across the room, Lola stirred in her seat and pinned me down with smoldering eyes. I saw Pit Bull's buddies passing notes. I raised my right hand and shook it. With my left hand waving in front of my nose, I spluttered, "Can I go to the girls' room?"

Ms. Yolanda paused and flicked her eyes towards me.

"*May* I go to the girls' room?" she corrected me.

"May I go to the girls' room?" I asked.

"Yes, you may."

I got up from my seat. Doubled over, I clutched my stomach, dashed up to Ms. Yolanda's desk and grabbed the hall pass before running out of the classroom. I saw Lola's grin, her too-white teeth showing, making her look more like a dog's snarl than a grin. I rushed past her, out into the darkened hallway.

I sped across the hallway and pushed opened the girls' room door. Sucking in some clean air, I darted inside and made it to the sink, grasping my left side. I dry-heaved into the cracked ceramic bowl. My eyes watered. My nose numbed out. I shuddered as waves of chills spread through my belly, arms, and feet. After three painful spasms my nausea calmed down.

I turned on the faucet and drew a brown paper towel from the dispenser. Wetting it beneath the faucet, I let the cold water soak through it. I wiped my face, neck, and hands. Leaning against the sink, I waited for my heart to stop thudding. I checked my watch. It read eight-thirty. The spray-painted graffiti walls mocked me. The foul odor of the stale cigarettes did nothing for my stomach. It kept rolling and tilting. I waited three more minutes. Each time I soaked the coarse brown paper and held it to my lips, my cheeks, and my forehead.

My stomach stopped heaving. I cupped my hands and took a quick drink from the faucet. Ugh! It tasted worse than the ground water we drank at home. This time the water stayed down without my spitting it back up or rising in my throat. I turned off the faucet and left the girls' room. I had to get back to class.

Pit Bull blocked my way. He bared his teeth, growled, crouched and lunged towards me. I backed up into the hallway wall. At five foot nine inches tall, Pit Bull towered over me. He leaned against the wall, both of his large hands trapping me between them. His head stuck out like a vulture's. "Going somewhere?"

I squirmed against the wall, praying to blend into it. His garlic breath bathed me in waves. My stomach pitched. My lips twisted. I forced my words out, each one stumbling over the next one.

"Ba—back to class. What—what about you?"

My voice froze. I tried slipping underneath his armpits, but his legs straddled mine. I was forced back against the wall, wedged and trapped, like this morning's encounter with the black fist.

"Not so fast, girlie."

His breath stank of stale cigarette smoke. I turned my head to one side. Pit Bull moved his head so his face remained lined up with mine. "I ain't finished with you yet."

He leaned closer into me. He parted his lips. I felt his hot breath on my face. His chest heaved.

"Am I interrupting something?"

Pit Bull twisted his head and stared. I looked past his head. We both saw Principal Teddy standing behind him. Pit Bull swallowed and stopped leaning against the wall, as if he'd just finished doing pushups.

"I...I was just asking her if she had a nice summer."

I saw Principal Teddy's eyes travel up and down Pit Bull's jersey and his pants. "You know how I feel about sagging pants, son. Why don't you go to my office and change? I've got some sweats that might fit you. Go on."

Pit Bull managed a weak smile.

"I forgot."

"Who's your teacher?"

"Ms. Yolanda," I said.

Principal Teddy stared past Pit Bull and focused on me. "And you are?"

"Anna Mae Botts." I waved the hall pass in front of the principal's eyes. "I was going back to class when Stanley ran into me. He's in my homeroom class this year." I added that more for Pit Bull's sake than for Principal Teddy's.

"Stanley, go to my office and change. I expect you in Ms. Yolanda's class by eight forty-five. If you're not in class by then I'll call your father!"

Stanley marched down the hall toward Principal Teddy's school office. Principal Teddy studied me.

"Anna Mae, you have a brother, Malcolm. I met him in the hallway this morning, running. Let's go back to Ms. Yolanda's class and see what she says about your trip to the girls' room."

Principal Teddy walked me back to class. I entered the room and went to my seat. Ms. Yolanda smiled at the principal. He walked up to her desk. She stood up. They turned their backs to the class.

"What happened to you?" Raul whispered.

"Pit Bull happened. He's still mad from this morning. The principal had to step in between us."

I felt Lola's glance. Her gaze burned through my blouse. She held up two fingers. One crossed the other like a crucifix. I dropped my eyes and studied my desktop. Raul stopped talking, but I knew he was worried about me.

Principal Teddy and Ms. Yolanda spoke for three more minutes. She escorted the principal to the door. The last two words I heard her say were. "About Stanley..."

I never heard the rest of Ms. Yolanda's sentence. It faded as I watched a piece of red chalk rise from the blackboard shelf. It rested in mid-air and settled close to the board. The chalk straightened. With its pointed end, it scratched and squealed as it wrote three sentences on it.

Neither Ms. Yolanda nor Principal Teddy paid any attention to it. Neither of them turned as the chalk howled and wrote its jagged message.

I saw Lola cover her ears, as did most of the class. Three of Pit Bull's posse— Mark, John and Joey—stood up from their desks and crept forward. The chalk flew across the room. All three backed down and seated themselves. They flung their arms in front of their faces.

Their heads ducked behind them. The chalk hovered in mid-air. I watched it. It remained by Mark's desk. He cringed and slid down into his seat until only his head and shoulders remained visible. Lola watched, open-mouthed. Her tongue flickered out. I couldn't decide if she would scream or not. The gum fell to the floor. Raul leaned forward and whispered, "Just like the fist."

I nodded and studied the chalk. It moved away from Mark's desk and traveled towards me. Compelled, I stood up, my hand outstretched. The chalk fell into my palm. I sat down. Ms. Yolanda and Principal Teddy shook hands. Principal Teddy left. Ms. Yolanda walked back to her desk.

"No more interruptions. Anna Mae, read your paper please."

I picked up my unfinished assignment and recited about the great scooter adventure Malcolm and I had in July. Raul laughed and clapped his hands. Christine giggled. The class joined in, all except Lola Simms and Pit Bull's friends. They sat there, stone-faced, with their arms crossed against their chests. Ms. Yolanda congratulated me on an amusing story.

At eight forty-nine Pit Bull sauntered into class, wearing blue and white sweat pants and a hooded sweat jacket with the number "eight" printed on it. His sweat pants sported two red racing stripes down the side of the legs. His girlfriend, Lola, beamed. I watched as Pit Bull dropped into the now-vacant desk-chair.

He angled his head and read off the board. "Send her home. The gold isn't here."

Ms. Yolanda froze. She held the ruler in mid-air.

"What did you say?" She aimed the question at Pit Bull.

"I read, 'Send her home. The gold isn't here.' Isn't that part of the lesson?" Pit Bull grimaced.

He exchanged puzzled glances with Ms. Yolanda. The class stared at the board. I felt the chalk shake in my palm like a Mexican jumping bean. Making a fist, I bent over and tucked it into my sneaker, under my heel.

Ms. Yolanda studied the board. "Who wrote this?"

No one answered. Ms. Yolanda picked up her notebook. "Raul Garcia, do you know who wrote those sentences on the board?"

"No, Ms. Yolanda, I didn't see anyone at the board writing."

Ms. Yolanda put down her notebook. She leaned over the desk and stared at Raul. She held his gaze. I expected her to pounce on him. "You saw no one?"

"Yes, Ma'am, I saw no one."

Ms. Yolanda dropped her glare first. Raul glanced back at me. His lips half parted as if to add something in his defense. Ms. Yolanda stared at the board. Her lips moved. Lola Simms stood up by her desk. In a loud voice, she accused me. "I know who wrote those sentences on the board, Ms. Yolanda. It was Anna Mae Botts!"

I shook my head, denying the charge. Ms. Yolanda's eyes widened. "Have I been deceived?" She rested her hands flat on the desk and rose halfway. "Anna Mae Botts, go stand in the corner. Lola Simms, go stand in the opposite corner, facing the wall."

Ms. Yolanda settled back into her seat. I saw her pick up her notebook as she looked back at the class. "Now, let's finish the assignment before something else happens. Then I'll pass out the class schedules and your history books. There'll be enough time for y'all to get to your second period class!"

I heard a unified gasp. I knew it wasn't from Ms. Yolanda's announcement. I shifted my eyes sideways and then I stared at the blackboard. I couldn't believe what I saw. An eraser rose from the blackboard shelf and positioned itself by the first sentence. One corner rested on the board. The eraser removed it from the board, and then dropped onto the shelf.

During this exercise, Ms. Yolanda explained the impromptu assignment to Pit Bull. I didn't hear Pit Bull's answer, but whatever he said, the class whistled and stomped their feet. I heard the ruler crack against Ms. Yolanda's desk. The class subsided. Pit Bull must've made up something on the spot. I heard his monotone voice tell a story that he had used last year, in sixth grade.

When he stopped speaking, I heard Ms. Yolanda's high-heeled shoes squeal as she turned towards the board. I watched her, through slit eyes. Her mouth hung open. I guess she must have seen the remaining two sentences. She stepped up to the board and touched it with her forefinger.

It jerked back. She screamed and retreated. Three other sentences popped up on the board. Her eyes widened. For some unknown reason, I snapped my fingers. She didn't budge. I tested her further and left the corner. Ms. Yolanda never said a word. I walked up to her and clapped my hands up close to her ears. Nothing! Her face remained passive.

The other kids remained seated and fidgeted. Pit Bull glared at me. Lola left her corner and joined Pit Bull at his desk. She leaned forward and cupped her ear. He whispered something. Their harsh voices grated. Lola raised her baby blue eyes towards me and laughed. Shivers ran up and down my spine. I didn't like the way she smirked, but I refused to fight her. I had something else in mind.

I felt my heel heave. The chalk leaped out of my sneaker and sped up to the board. It settled on the shelf next to the eraser.

Raul rose from his desk. He joined me in the corner and eyed the remaining sentences on the board. "What do they refer to?"

I checked the board. "'Go to Chennault Plantation. The gold is buried there. Davis owes us money!'"

"Not sure. It makes as much sense as it did this morning," I said.

"What does?" Pit Bull asked, jumping in with both feet. He left his desk. Lola trailed behind him. "What aren't you telling us?" Pit Bull asked.

The rest of the class stared at Ms. Yolanda, waiting for her to do something. The Asians and Hispanics milled at the back of the room. The blacks loitered by their desks and exchanged written notes. The white kids—the "adventurers"—were the only ones who took advantage of Ms. Yolanda's frozen stance. The only thing I saw moving was her chest, rising and falling. Otherwise, Ms. Yolanda wasn't really there in that classroom with us. I didn't know what to do. Her body was there, but her self was gone.

Raul inched closer to me. Pit Bull made a sudden move. He pushed Raul away from me. "Out of my way, Burrito Man, if ya know what's good for you. About this morning, what did that thingy want?"

"I don't know what *thingy* you mean," I lied.

Pit Bull frowned and shoved me. Lola grabbed my arm and jerked it. Raul pushed Lola away from me and sucker-punched Pit Bull. Ms. Yolanda stirred.

"What is going on? Anna Mae Botts, Lola Simms, go back to your corners. Raul Garcia and Stanley Paxton, stop fighting or I'll have both of you suspended. No more interruptions, if you please. Principal Teddy is just a phone call away! Now, settle down!"

The first bell rang for second period.

I stood in the corner, my face burning. Raul fled back to his desk and hauled his backpack from under the seat. Pit Bull shrugged and dragged Lola from her corner. They argued as they retreated from the room. Ms. Yolanda shook the ruler at them, but they fled. Outside, in the hallway, I heard their laughter. The rest of Pit Bull's gang filed out. Once all the whites had left the classroom, the rest of the class filed out after them, the blacks first, followed by the Hispanics and Asians. I remained behind, waiting for Ms. Yolanda to excuse me.

I peeked at the board. The written sentences were gone. In their place, something else emerged. Straining my eyes, I saw a faint outline of a man's torso appear on the blackboard. The blackboard gave the man a solid appearance. Across his chest, a wooden board rested. It hung from two link chains that were fitted around the man's neck. Crude burned letters spelled out my name. It read, "A-N-N-A M-A-E, GO TO CHENNAULT PLANTATION!"

I heard a deep chuckle.

Chapter Three

Raul stood by the door. He held my backpack by its straps. It dangled Ms. Yolanda looked up and stared at it, as if mesmerized. She watched it for four or five seconds, and then made up her mind. Her voice drifted towards me.

"Are you still there? Mr. Wong, your geometry teacher, dislikes students who meander in late. You'd better hoof it."

I broke wind. Raul giggled. He threw my backpack at me. It landed at my feet with an *oof*. Ms. Yolanda buried her face in her hands. I took that as a signal to leave. Raul pushed the door open and I sailed through it, Raul at my heels.

The rest of the day went by in a blur. I kept looking for something to appear. It did, right after lunch. Principal Teddy paid my geometry class a visit. In his left hand he held something by its tendril. I sank lower into my seat. Footsteps echoed on the scuffed tile flooring. They halted by my chair-desk.

I peered down and saw two large black-laced, polished oxford shoes, the same kind my Poppa wore to work as a patrolman. My heart sank. I pressed my right hand over my chest. The sharp pricks lasted a split second, but I ached all over as if a farm tractor had stalled on my chest.

Principal Teddy's pressed black suit pants smelled of camphor. I waited for the axe to fall.

"Is this yours?"

The principal shoved the ginger root under my nose. I wheezed and coughed. My eyes watered. I tilted my head and locked eyes with him.

"Yeah, sort of," I whispered.

"Do you know what this is?"

The interrogation continued. I squirmed in my seat. Textbooks shuffled on top of the other students' desks. Text pages crackled as the rest of the class studied their pending homework assignments. Principal Teddy bent over. His two hands rested flat on my desk. Lowering his head, I watched his lips form the words I dreaded hearing.

"See me after school, Ms. Botts."

I wanted to disappear. Mr. Wong cleared his throat— a thin raspy sound. Principal Teddy marched off and left me defeated at my desk. Raul reached over and patted my shoulder.

"I'll wait for you."

"Class, come to order," Mr. Wong said in a sing-song tone.

The rest of the class stopped rattling their pens, papers, and geometry workbooks. Mr. Wong walked up to the board and wrote out our homework assignment. The rest of the 45-minute period was spent learning the five major principles of geometry.

The first warning bell for my next class couldn't come fast enough. I charged out of the room. I left Raul behind somewhere between his desk-chair and the doorway. Out of breath, I waited by the water fountain. He soon joined me. For the second time that day, Raul threw my backpack at me.

"Going somewhere?"

I shook my head.

"Had to get out of there fast. It didn't smell right."

"Oh, yeah, ya forget this in your mad rush."

Raul threw the ginger root at me. I caught it.

"Where didja find it?"

"Where Principal Teddy left it...on your desktop!"

I gulped.

"Didn't see it. I was busy."

"Let's go. First the black fist, then the flying chalk and eraser, and now this... Got anything else up your sleeve you're not tellin' me about?"

I picked up my backpack and thrust the ginger root in my skirt pocket. The second bell rang. Raul took my hand and pushed me forward. Three hallways and one stairwell later we made it to our next class: music appreciation. My schedule of classes soon filled up my mind.

The teachers distributed their text and workbooks: general science, English, Social Studies, gym, home economics, and art classes. We got lectured on personal hygiene, frogs, diagramming grammar, and learning notes. Sometimes I caught my teachers watching me, as if they expected me to start a fight or disrupt the class.

The story of the black fist, flying chalk, floating erasers and the ginger root followed me everywhere. The eighth-grade boys slapped me on the back. The girls giggled or avoided me as if I didn't exist. The other seventh graders hid behind their textbooks and peeked over them. The adventurers were the worst.

With Pit Bull and Lola egging them on, the white students threw spitballs or tripped me as I walked past them. Raul did what he could, but the school rules and regulations hemmed us in. No fist fights. No scuffling. No shoving. No running. I waited to see when the No breathing sign would go up alongside the other no-no's.

Raul suspected that Ms. Yolanda and Principal Teddy had phoned ahead, using the intercom between the classrooms to warn my other teachers. Whenever one of my teachers glanced up at me, I sat motionless, like a doe exposed in front of a car's headlights.

At last the day was over. Raul and I had returned to Ms. Yolanda's homeroom. The bell rang fifteen minutes later, signaling the end of school. Thank God, the first day had come to an end. I didn't think I would make it. I wouldn't have if it hadn't been for Raul. He pulled me through.

Pit Bull and Lola Simms, hand-in-hand, ran out of class before Ms. Yolanda could stop them. The rest of their gang followed behind, but not before they pulled their eye sockets down on their cheeks and stuck their tongues out at me.

I sighed and ignored them. Making eye contact with them only made things worse, and I had had enough for one day. Picking up my backpack, I waited for Raul as he hefted his backpack on his shoulders. Prickles raced up and down my back, a sure sign that something else was about to happen, but nothing did. I turned and faced Ms. Yolanda. She smiled. "See you tomorrow, Anna Mae, Raul. Let's hope it's a bit quieter, shall we?"

I nodded. Raul grabbed my arm and we strolled out of class. In the hallway, Raul lowered his hand. "It's been fun. Too bad it's another three months until Thanksgiving!" He peered into my face. He whipped out his handkerchief and handed it to me.

"You weren't supposed to see that."

He shrugged.

"What a day! I don't think I can take another one like today. Let's get outta here."

Raul smiled.

"Shouldn't Malcolm be here by now?"

I smacked my forehead.

"Darn! Malcolm's already home. Third grade let out 30 minutes ago."

"Lucky stiff."

I wiped my eyes.

"I'll race you home."

"Yar on!"

Malcolm met me at the front door when I let myself in. Dust coated his cropped black hair. Behind him, instead of Momma, I saw Granma Zora.

"Granma, wha' are ya doin' here?"

"Yar Momma ask me t' come and stay with ya a spell. Said she needed me t' help out with the lot of yo'. Yar Poppa paid for my bus ticket, and here I be. Yar Poppa come home early from work and took yo' Momma t' Atlanta for their twenty-year college reunion. I came 'fore they left."

I stared, my mouth wide open. I clean forgot that Poppa hinted that he and Momma would go away for the week. He even said that Granma was coming for a visit, but I thought it was his momma, not my momma's momma.

Granma looked awesome. She wore a bright blue turban with a turkey feather sticking out at one end. She held a vacuum cleaner in her yellow rubber-gloved right hand. Over a green t-shirt Granma wore a brown cleaning apron. "Anna Mae, get yo'self back t' the shed, the one yo' Daddy built for company. Yo' be sleepin' there 'til I goes in the sprin'."

"In the sprin'?"

"Didn't yo' Momma tell you nothin'? I'm gonna live here with you 'til sprin' cause I get lonely on the island durin' the winter. Yo' Momma knows that. I told 'em I keep the house and you and Malcolm clean. Y'all way too big for doin' nothin'. Time for y'all t' start helpin' out."

I glanced at Malcolm. He shifted his eyes, first from me, then at Granma, and then at the floor.

"Here, take this mojo and say aftah me..."

I stared at the still object Granma laid in my hand. It reminded me of what was left of a chicken. I brought it up to my nose and sniffed, then I gagged and coughed. I bent over double.

"Granma, this is a dead..."

I never got to finish my sentence. Granma huffed and puffed. I thought she'd blow me down. She snatched the carcass out of my hand and turned on her heel. She hurried towards the kitchen. Malcolm and I followed behind. The kitchen door swung open. I reached for it and held the door with my left hand. Malcolm ducked under my arm.

"She's over here. Granma?"

I trotted into the kitchen and saw Granma Zora seize a carving knife from the knife block. She plunged it into the linoleum. It cracked apart. Underneath, the plywood floor splintered. Granma looked up. She wet her lips.

"Dig!"

Malcolm fell to his knees and slammed his fist into the broken floor. The wood split apart. Hard-packed dirt was underneath. I ran to the silver drawer and took out an oval-shaped serving spoon.

"Here!"

I handed the spoon to Malcolm. He grunted and grabbed the spoon with both hands. Malcolm raised the spoon up into the air, and then brought it down, smacking the dirt. I thought it would bend from the impact, but it didn't.

Malcolm kept digging. The hole got larger and deeper. Granma wheezed beside him. She held the dead thing in her hands. She blew on it from time to time, muttering incoherent words. I watched, but I said nothing.

Ten minutes passed by.

"That's enough," Granma said. "Bury it!"

Malcolm took the foul-smelling carcass from her. He dropped it into the hole. Granma laid her hands on it and muttered a spell. I didn't catch all of it. Bits and pieces I caught—stone, protect, desire, greed, jealousy, hate—words I didn't think Granma knew much about.

Once she finished singing, Granma ripped the spoon from Malcolm's hand and shoveled the dirt over the mess. Five minutes later, she pounded and smoothed the dirt over her conjure. Back went the wood, or what was left of it. Granma grabbed the cracked linoleum piece and stuck it back in place.

"Git the glue. It's in the garage."

Malcolm ran out through the rear kitchen door that led to the garage. He returned with the wood glue. Granma snatched it from him. She crushed the two sides of the plastic glue bottle together. The glue oozed out of its spout.

Granma picked up one corner of the linoleum and smeared the glue on its back. She laid it back down.

"Stomp on it," she ordered.

Malcolm got to his feet and stomped both feet on the tile piece. Granma watched. She never took her eyes off of him. I waited three minutes. The sweat dripped off of me, soaking my blouse.

"Are ya through?"

Granma lifted her eyes.

"Yes, chile, we're through. Don' wan' yo and yar brothahh harm in any way while yo Poppa and Momma not here t' protect ya. Now, we kin clean this here house 'til it glows. We'll rest aftah that. Get goin', chile. We don't have all day."

Granma pushed herself up off the floor and headed towards the shed. You had to go through my bedroom to get to the shed. Poppa built it as an afterthought when we needed the extra space to store stuff in the house and the basement and the garage got too cluttered.

All of my school uniforms lay scattered on my bed. My shoes were thrown helter-skelter into the closet. My blankets, pillows, and sheets were piled on top of my clothes.

The room stunk of skunk. I opened the closet door and peered in. The wooden shelves were bare. A few wire hangers hung from the metal bar Poppa used when he did chin-ups, but now he no longer bothered doing them. Hanging next to Poppa's things, a bulging white cotton bag, tied with a blue ribbon, dangled. I reached out and cradled the bag with both hands. The ribbon untied itself. I sniffed, and then peered in. I saw sunflower seeds, bay leaves, and what looked like pieces of skunk cabbage. Taking my forefinger, I poked at the mixture. Tears welled up in my eyes. I couldn't believe what else I saw: three strands of my hair, a blood-stained tissue from when my nose bled last week, a strip of denim from my denim jacket, and my lost hair comb.

A piece of paper rose to the surface. On it I saw Granma's spidery longhand. It read "Mix equal parts of these ingredients togethah on a Saturday when de moon is Full. Keep dis bag close. It will protect yo' from the debil 'emself."

Bile rose at the back of my throat. I dropped the bag and yelled. "Granma!"

I backed out of the closet until I fell backwards on my bed. Malcolm rushed in with a chocolate mustache over his lips and an oatmeal cookie in one hand.

"She sent me. What's up?"

I pointed at the closet. He tiptoed up to it and peeked in.

"I don't...oh...yuk...what is that smell?"

Again, I pointed at the closet. This time I aimed my finger at the floor. He stooped over. I heard him hiccup.

"Yuk! What is that stuff?"

"Ask her. No! Wait, I'll ask her. You stay here."

"Not on your life," Malcolm said.

He dashed out of the room first. I followed and slammed the connecting door between my room and the shed. It didn't shut tight all the way. The door was crooked because of the humidity. Lowery, Georgia was damp in the spring and fall. Snow didn't fall much here because we were too far south.

In the kitchen, Granma turned and straightened.

"Yo called?"

"Wha' is tha' thingy smellin' up my room?"

"Thingy?"

Granma scowled, glaring at me.

"No sense gettin' mad. Jest tryin' t'protect yo' from evil spirits. And tha's the thanks I get? Nevah could undahstand how yo' Momma could raise such a young'un like yo' without givin' yo' a heap of sense."

"I don' need anothahh mojo. Yar here now."

Granma snuffled.

"Is tha' all tha's botherin' yo'? Go git yoself int' yar workin' clothes, othahhwise we ain't gonna git nothin' done t'day."

I ran from the kitchen, back into the shed. Kicking the door shut, I tore off my white button-down blouse, dark navy skirt, and put on my worn jeans and a white t-shirt. Mama demanded that we wear slippers inside the house, so I shoved on my flip-flops. They were easier on my feet than stupid slippers.

Sighing, I walked back to the kitchen. Granma sat at the table, watching Malcolm eat. It was a full-time job, since Malcolm ate all the time. Her thick lips turned downwards. I braced myself for the grilling I knew was coming because of "big mouth Malcolm." Sure enough, Granma gave me the first degree.

"Yo' little brothahh tells me you saw a haint in the school yard this mornin'."

"Not a haint, granma, a black fist. It jus' floated."

Her eyes widened. I thought maybe she was scared, but no such luck.

"Ya lyin' t' me, chile?"

"No. A friend from last year saw it, too, and so did Pit Bull."

"Pit Bull?" Granma asked.

"His real name is Stanley Paxton."

"Is tha' a fact? Yo' think tha's the same black hand I saw when I was a young'un? I suppose yo' tellin' the truth."

That stopped me short. I stared at her as if I hadn't heard her right.

"When yo' was a chile, Granma?"

She stared right through me. It gave me the creeps. It was as if I wasn't in that room, like she spoke to herself or Momma when Momma was a little girl.

"Funny things happened t' me when I was little. Young'uns stayed away, but my Momma knew I was somthin' else. I saw thin's that othahh people didn't."

My goose bumps returned. I felt lightheaded, as if I'd sniffed too much of Momma's vanilla perfume. The words fell out of my mouth.

"It was real. I swear on the family Bible."

"Of course yo' do," Granma soothed me as best she could. "Yo' Momma says yo' tell tales. It's the same as lyin'."

I twisted my hands. Granma watched me. I tried stopping them, but they had a life of their own. Out came some more fibs, or at least I was sure that was what Granma thought. They flowed out before I could stop them.

"A black fist blocked Raul, Malcolm and me from getting into school. Pit Bull saw it, but he would never admit to it. I ain't takin' back my words."

I glared at her. Granma laughed, an eerie, shrill noise that sounded a lot like chalk scratching the wrong way on a blackboard. I shivered.

"We'll see if yo' have the sight or not,"

Granma's eyes seared through me as if she burned the skin off of my chest. I hated it when she looked at me that way. It meant that she thought I was lying to her. It didn't matter what I said or did to defend myself, even when I offered to swear on the family Bible, not that I believed that would help. What could I do to convince her?

I knew Granma wasn't done with me. She cleared her throat and folded her arms in front of her chest. I waited, wondering when the next salvo would shoot out. I didn't have to wait very long.

"Malcolm tells me he wetted 'emself this mornin'. Said it was Raul Garcia's fault. The Mexican told him t' cross his legs. Next time y'all tell Raul to keep his mouth shut. If Malcolm needs t' go, then Malcolm goes. If y'alls friend can' keep his tongue still, then he can' be friends with yo'. Yo' Daddy and Momma asked me t' take care of y'all. I won't have 'em tellin' my young'uns wha' t' do."

"It wasn' like tha', Granma. I told Malcolm t' git lost, not Raul. It was me."

"If yo' say so. Let's git goin'. This ole house needs cleanin' somethin' bad. Go get that shed put togethah right so it ain't no pig sty. Dust the room and put towels in the bathroom. Malcolm and I will git the front rooms. Yo' 'bout finished?"

Malcolm stopped eating. Cookie crumbs sprinkled the tabletop. His napkin lay crumbled up next to his empty glass of milk. When Granma spoke, Malcolm melted into the background. He knew enough when to keep quiet and small.

Granma took a deep breath. Before she said anything else, I rushed in, flapping my mouth. "I'll take care of it all. It will get done." I gabbled the words before I'd thought about them. Malcolm's eyes rounded. Granma slapped the tabletop with palms flat.

"Don't mess with me, Anna Mae. Yo' gettin' t' big for yo' breeches since yo' gone into seventh grade. Watch yo' lips, chile. They've gotta life of their own."

I held my breath and waited for her to say something else, but it never came.

"My throat is dry as a day-old hide alayin' in the sun. How 'bout some ice cold lemonade, and then yo' tidy up the shed aftah?"

Malcolm pushed his chair away from the table. He stood up, his eyes blank.

"Be right back."

He ran from the room. The room grew cold. Granma shoved her chair away from the table.

"Stay put. Somethin' ain't right."

She hurried after Malcolm. I cocked my head and listened. I didn't hear either one of them. At seventy,

Granma could move when she wanted to. I strained my ears. The house became still. I could hear the air conditioner turn on and water flow into the pipes. They gurgled. I heard the kitchen faucet dripping. I clamped my hands to my ears, but the drip, drip, drip of the faucet increased its loudness. The noise went through my hands.

I heard someone stomping, and I thought it was Malcolm fooling around. I sniffed the air. The scent of lavender and roses invaded the hallway. I retreated into the living room and looked around. My eyes centered on the window that faced the neighbor's hedge.

The window frosted over. Letters dripped on the glass like melting icicles, ragged and blurred. A cold black hand covered my mouth. I stiffened. My eyes swung to the other side of the room. In the far corner, a mist twisted. Time stretched out endlessly. I strained my ears, but I heard nothing.

Then I saw him. An officer dressed in a gray uniform with golden buttons, high black boots and silver spurs. He glided towards me, but he faded when he reached me.

I bit the hand. It jerked away. My lips burned. I screamed, "Granma!"

I must have fainted. When I came to, Granma and Malcolm were kneeling on the floor beside me.

"Wha' happened?" Granma asked.

"She saw anothah haint," Malcolm said, wiping my forehead with a damp bathroom towel.

Granma glared. "No haints live here, oh dear Jesus. Tha' why I done made tha' mojo. Don' eveah let me hear yo' sayin' that 'gain."

"Wha'evah," Malcolm said.

"Anna Mae, wha' happened t' yo'?"

"It started with the window. It frosted ovah. Written letters 'peared on it."

She narrowed her eyes and clambered back to her feet. Granma pushed past the sofa and crept to the window. I saw her eyes. They widened until you could see her brown pupils. She studied the window, reached up and touched it. "The window's wet, but I reckon. I don' see any lettah spellin' words. Yo' sure 'bout tha'?"

Malcolm helped me to my feet. I trembled a bit, but kept my balance.

"Granma, look!" Malcolm pointed. On the window, letters appeared. My name, Anna Mae, was spelled out. Malcolm ran over. He traced the letters with his fingertips. "Cool!"

Granma looked at the window, and then swung her eyes towards me. "Wha' are yo' goin' t' do 'bout it?"

I looked at her. "Yo' see my name?"

"Of course, chile. Wha' I want to know is wha' are yo'goin' t' do 'bout it?"

"I'm not sure. First yo' 'cuse me of lyin' and now yo'r not. Wha' gives?"

"Lost gold."

Granma said it so plainly that I thought I heard her wrong.

"Whose lost gold?"

Granma stamped her foot. "The black fist's lost gold. Child, yo' ain't been paying 'tention t' nothin' I been sayin'. Wha' are yo' goin' t' do 'bout it?"

"Why are yo' hollerin' at me? I'm doin' the best I can. This is new t' me. I need t' think first, 'fore I act."

"Don' take t' long. Someone else might figurah it out afore yo', then wha' will yo' do?"

Malcolm turned his head back and forth between the two of us. He was confused. So was I. Why didn't Granma find the gold if she was so hot to trot for it? I turned and walked towards the kitchen. "Yo' still thirsty, Granma?"

"Changin' the subject? I reckon the lemonade still sounds good. Malcolm, yo' want some too?"

"Anna Mae," Malcolm screeched. "Look at it...on the living room window. Dang, I thought that chicken hoodoo worked!"

"False bottoms!" was written on the window.

"Merciful heavens!" Granma shouted. Her hands flew up over her eyes and covered them.

"It's meltin'" Malcolm howled. "See? Cat prints on the glass."

Granma backed up and sat on the sofa. She stroked her throat.

"Bettah write down wha' yo see 'fore it is gone. Malcolm, run int' yo' Poppa's den and get yo' sistah a slip of paper and pencil so she can write 'em down."

Malcolm ran down the hallway. I heard Poppa's study door open and then close. Malcolm rushed back into the room with a yellow-lined pad and a pencil stub. He licked the stub and handed both over to me. I wrote down what I saw.

I felt Granma's eyes watching me.

"Got 'em, "I said.

"Let's have our lemonade 'fore the haint comes back!"

Chapter Four

Wednesday

The next morning I met Raul at the railroad tracks. Malcolm lagged behind me. The GDOT had recently upgraded these tracks so Amtrak could run their Crescent trains from New York City via Washington D.C., through Lowry and on to Atlanta. The train disgorged its passengers in New Orleans—its final destination.

I watched as Raul's gaze devoured the tracks. He loved trains and if I would let him, he would spend hours walking the rails as far north as Athens. I shaded my eyes and looked at Malcolm. He mimicked Raul, his hero, whenever he could. Soon Malcolm would join Raul by the tracks, bend over, reach out and touch the rails. The look in his eyes was far away as Malcolm saw the old steam trains spouting billowing smoke and running at fifteen miles an hour.

I stepped on the wooden tiers between the metal tracks and waited on the far side. Both Raul and Malcolm stood side by side, lost in thought, imagining, I guess, white- haired men wearing caps and waving lanterns to the engineers who were sitting in the main engine.

"Come on, will yo'? I don' want a repeat performance like yesterday."

I tapped my feet on the road. Raul looked up first and sauntered to my side of the tracks. Malcolm trod behind, hot on his heels.

"Wanna eat over at my house tonight?" Raul asked.

"Sure, why not. Granma and Malcolm can get 'long without me."

Malcolm struck his classic pose—arms bent, fists on hips—and he pouted.

"Yo' didn' ask me. Why can' I come too?"

"Yo' way too young," I said.

Raul glanced at Malcolm and winked. "Abuelita and Abuelito won't believe you. I tried tellin' 'em what happened yesterday out in the schoolyard and then in Ms. Yolanda's class. They thought I was makin' it up. Abuelito's face turned fire-engine red. Abuelita stroked her Ankh. It's a amulet she wears 'round her throat. They didn't outright call me a liar, but they came real close to it. I told 'em yo' would tell 'em what happened. They'll believe you, Anna Mae!"

Raul's eyes teared up. I looked down at the ground and hugged myself. Malcolm glared at me. "You mean somethin' else happened when I wasn' there? You could've said somthin' to me. I ain't a baby."

"A piece of chalk wrote on the blackboard by itself. An eraser wiped the board clean. You saw how Granma acted yesterday afternoon. I couldn't say nothin' then."

"Tell me now," Malcolm demanded

"I tole you. Ms. Yolanda and Principal Teddy nevah saw it."

"And you didn't tell me? Nothin' like that happened in my class. Señor Santos would've a fit first."

"That's not all," Raul said. "Pit Bull saw it too...the black fist. It attacked him!"

Malcolm's mouth dropped opened. I pulled at Raul's arm, but I aimed my eyes at Malcolm.

"We bettah get movin' if we're t' make it by eight."

Neither Malcolm nor Raul argued with me. The black fist attack and blockage was just too fresh in our minds. We just barely made it to school by first bell. Malcolm scurried to the elementary school side, while Raul and I darted into the main door of the school. Pit Bull, Lola, and their friends blocked the middle of the hallway. As far as I could see, there was no way to get around them. Raul and I had to plow through them. Pit Bull spotted us first.

"I see you found Burrito Boy."

He laughed.

"Come on, Raul," I said.

I shoved my way through the throng. Raul followed, but not fast enough. The next thing I knew, Raul grabbed my arm. He toppled to the side and pulled me down on top of him. We collapsed in a heap on the floor.

Lola smirked and flounced off. Pit Bull followed. His friends kicked my backpack as they stepped over us. Raul forced my head to the floor.

"Lie flat," he hissed.

It felt like the rest of the kids from our homeroom used us as an exercise mat. Thirty seconds must have passed before I lifted my head. The hallway was cleared by then. I scooted to my feet. Finally, Raul stood too. He brushed his navy blue pants with his hand. Some of the dirt came off, but not all of it. Raul swatted at my skirt. It helped some, but some dust clung to the fabric.

"I hate 'em!" I said.

Raul shrugged. "He's not worth it. Jest stay outta his way."

We walked into homeroom together. Raul took the lead, and I followed him to our desk-chairs. We stowed our backpacks under our chairs, and then sat down. Pit Bull and Lola hadn't made it in yet. The third and final bell rang. The two of them strolled in like nothing mattered.

Pit Bull yawned and stuck out his tongue. Lola smoothed her hair, blouse, and skirt. The rest of their gang sauntered to their desks and sat down. All of them reeked of cigarette smoke; I even saw a pack rolled up in one of Pit Bull's short tee-shirt sleeves. Ms. Yolanda pretended not to notice.

The rest of the class waited while Pit Bull, Lola and their friends settled in. Catherine waved to Lola. Wendy smiled at Pit Bull. Ms. Yolanda stood in front of her desk and leaned against it. She didn't greet anyone; she just stood in front of desk with her arms folded across her chest as if she was waiting for something.

I held my breath. Ms. Yolanda stood up and walked to the door. She closed it with a thud and then returned to her desk. She held up her roll-call book and started calling out the names. When my name was called, I stuck my hand up. Something brushed my fingertips. I glanced up. A lighted match's flame blew towards the fire sprinkler. Around the sprinkler, I saw the faint outline of the black fist. It shimmered from the heat.

My eyes widened. Water splashed on my upturned face. The drip turned into a torrent of water. The sprinkler deluged me and Raul. The school's fire alarm tripped. Ms. Yolanda stopped speaking. She thumped her roll book on the desk and called out, "Everyone stand up!"

Soaked, I struggled from my desk-chair. I darted towards the door. From the doorway, I saw Raul untangle his legs from under his chair. I never heard Ms. Yolanda or Raul's cries. I crashed into Pit Bull. He blocked the door and kept his thick hand on its knob.

"Over here!"

Lola screamed. The gang rushed her and pushed her towards Pit Bull. I stood immobile, wedged in between Pit Bull and the second group of kids, pushing and shoving to get through. I gritted my teeth. With head bowed, I rammed Pit Bull from the back. His hand slipped from the knob. The door crashed opened. I fell into the hallway.

A ninth-grade hallway monitor gaped at me. She reached down and helped me to my feet. "Take it easy. You've got plenty of time. It's just a drill."

I hauled myself to my feet, but impatient, I refused to wait for the rest of my class.

I dashed down the hallway, pushing other students out of my way. Flying through the opened doors, catching my breath as I ran, I flung myself through and didn't rest until I came to the designated parking lot for guests, visitors and important dignitaries.

My chest heaving, I doubled over and saw other sneakers run towards me. I stopped heaving and looked up. Ms. Yolanda led the rest of my homeroom class single-file into the parking lot. Raul was with them. He turned his back when he saw me.

Half of the school retreated to the parking lot when the fire alarm sounded. The other half of the school—the elementary side—hadn't left the building.

Ms. Yolanda nodded when she spotted me. Raul stayed with the rest of the class. They shunned me. I hadn't thought of anyone but myself trying to get out of that wet room. I watched as Raul and the rest of the class waited with Ms. Yolanda. I noticed that my group consisted of Pit Bull, Lola Simms, their gang and me.

I turned my back on them and faced the street. The alarm kept clanging. I covered my ears. Ms. Yolanda did too. The entire middle school waited in the parking lot. I noticed, too, that Raul and I were the only ones soaked to the skin. The other middle-class students looked bone dry. That meant only our classroom's fire sprinkler had gone off. I shook my head and shivered. After ten minutes, the fire alarm stopped shrieking. I unclamped my ears and moved closer to Ms. Yolanda.

The fire chief and the police officers arrived five minutes later. Both vehicles parked in the emergency lanes that were set aside for that purpose. Disheveled, Principal Teddy joined the fire chief and a policewoman in the parking lot. They all shook hands.

With raised axes and clothed in oxygen helmets, rubber hip boots and gloves, the fire personnel ran through the main doors of the school building. Five minutes later, the fire chief poked his head out of Ms. Yolanda's classroom's window. He waved and disappeared.

I waited in agonized silence. Ms. Yolanda stood, her arms crossed and her eyes vacant. The fire chief and the firefighters returned. Everyone heard their verdict: "False alarm. No fire. There's water damage in one classroom. It's all clear. You can go back in now."

I glanced at Principal Teddy. His face was a mixture of relief and concern. "Did you reset the sprinkler?"

"We did," a female firefighter said.

Principal Teddy shook the fire chief's hand. I watched as the fire chief and the fire personnel climbed back up and into the fire engine. The engine roared to life as they left. The policewoman left in her squad car. The rest of the middle-school students filed back into school.

Ms. Yolanda herded our class back into a single line. She motioned for me to join in at the end of the line. Pit Bull, Lola Simms, and their gang edged closer, but they were a law unto themselves. They didn't step into line as I did.

Ms. Yolanda brought her hands up to her mouth and cupped them. "We're going to finish class in the gym this morning. This afternoon we'll use the auditorium. Follow me, and no talking."

My class walked towards the school. I whistled to Raul, but he ignored me; too busy gabbing with Catherine and Wendy. The class didn't use the main door. Instead, Ms. Yolanda took us to the side door that opened into a long covered hallway that connected the middle school with the elementary school.

Ms. Yolanda took the first flight of stairs after leaving the hallway, and led us down into the basement. I jerked as if something walked over my grave. I glanced at the worn cinderblocks and peeling green-painted walls. It reminded me of the drunk tank Poppa took my fourth grade class to visit in Lowry's jail as a warning not to drink too much.

Custodians were setting up school desks with attached seats when my class and I entered the room. The space smelled of day-old paint, turpentine, and gym sweat. The janitors left and returned with two large cartons. I watched as they opened the cartons with box cutters and scissors.

Ms. Yolanda interrupted my musings.

"Find a desk and sit down in the same order you sat in upstairs. I've asked the custodians to pass out your history workbooks so you can start working with them."

The class groaned. I found a desk in the middle of the room and sat down. I watched the other kids find desks similar to where they had sat upstairs. Pit Bull, I noticed, had trouble stuffing his large bulk into the desk-chair. Ms. Yolanda hid a grin and turned it into a yawn behind one hand.

Lola and the remaining gang members sat down, more or less surrounding Pit Bull. No one sat close to them.

Raul pushed a desk close to mine but made sure a good ten feet separated us.

Wendy threw a remaining workbook at me. I caught it in both hands. Pit Bull sneered. I lowered my eyes and concentrated on the workbook. It was thick and heavy. I opened to the first page when something stroked my leg. I looked down and froze. Underneath my desk, a burnt match rested. I stared until I thought my eyeballs would pop out.

I never saw or heard her coming. The next thing I knew, I saw a pair of dark blue high-heeled pumps. I tilted my head and looked up. Ms. Yolanda stood by my desk. "Am I disturbing you?"

I shook my head. My body turned cold. The nape hairs on the back of my neck stood up. Ms. Yolanda's lips pulled back. I started praying.

"Is there something you would like to share with the class?"

I leaned over and picked up the match. Ms. Yolanda stretched her hand out. I dropped it into her palm. She stood there, her eyes wide and bright. "Is that all?"

My voice quavered.

"Yes, Ma'am."

"Do you know how it got there?"

I shook my head. My face burned. I ran my tongue over my dried lips. My stomach flip-flopped. I saw two of everything as my eyes filled with tears. Sniffling, I rubbed my nose with the back of my hand. Ms. Yolanda turned her back and returned to her makeshift desk. I followed her with my eyes. No one spoke. Even Pit Bull kept quiet. Lola didn't waste her time on me. She smiled at Ms. Yolanda and sat tall, as if to say, "I'm the best student you've got." Numbed, I waited and watched.

Ms. Yolanda opened the drawer, dropped the match in, and closed it. She looked up and studied us. Clearing her throat, she addressed us. "Class, I want you to read the first two chapters of your history workbook and answer the first ten questions. Make sure you write a beginning, middle, and ending. When you're finished, you can read. I'm giving you an early recess. At eleven forty-five, you may leave for lunch, but be back in the auditorium by twelve-thirty. The rest of your classes will be taken with me."

The period stretched out forever. I yawned behind my history workbook. At eleven forty-five class was dismissed. Raul walked out with Christine Harper without waiting for Pit Bull, Lola and their crowd to leave first. I waited until all the kids—charity whites, blacks, Hispanics, and Asians—left the room.

I stared up at the gym sprinkler, but I saw no black fist. I scanned Ms. Yolanda's desk. A piece of chalk rested on the desk. It showed no signs of life. I was the last one to leave the gym room. Not even Ms. Yolanda said good-bye to me.

At twelve-thirty, still alone, I entered the auditorium. Ms. Yolanda met me at the door and pointed to a row of plush chairs. I noticed that the back seats were roped off. Everyone had to sit in the first two rows, whether they wanted to or not.

The rest of the students entered, gabbing. Raul sat on the opposite side of the auditorium, as far away from me as he could get. On stage, Ms. Yolanda stood behind a podium. She squinted back at us.

Ms. Yolanda reviewed our vocabulary words for science and reading. We spelled out each word in unison, as if we were attending a one-room schoolhouse. I noticed that Ms. Yolanda had her history textbook out. She opened it and stared straight at me.

"What do we remember about the Revolutionary War?"

No one raised their hands. For the next twenty minutes, Ms. Yolanda lectured us on the finer points of the Revolutionary War. She stepped out from behind the podium, grasping a stack of papers. She walked over to Wendy and handed her one stack, then she strode over to the opposite side of the auditorium and handed Raul the second stack of papers.

"Please take one each. They're quite thick, so handle them with care. When you've finished passing them out we'll discuss our term project for the school year."

I took one and passed on the remaining papers. Ms. Yolanda was right. The papers were stuck together with a large metal staple. I thumbed the pages and studied their contents. The first page read "Table of Contents." Underneath the title read the secondary title, "Myths and Tales of the War Between the States." I started reading out loud, drawn into a world I never knew existed.

"The War Between the States wasn't necessarily meant to free the slaves. In fact, when President Lincoln signed his Emancipation Proclamation he stated that it just happened to turn out that way."

Ms. Yolanda thumped the podium with her hand. "Anna Mae. I was telling the class that in seventh grade you study the first two years of the War Between the States. In tenth grade, you finish studying the rest of The War Between the States. Today, we're starting at the end because I'm more interested in your interpretation of the myths and legendary stories that are told about this war. Many of them have circulated in Georgia since the South lost the war. What do you think?"

I squirmed and nodded my head "yes" in agreement. My forehead beaded with sweat. I shifted in my chair and glanced at Raul. He turned his face away from me and faced Christine Harper. I dropped my eyes and clenched my fists.

Ms. Yolanda started lecturing again. This time I paid attention. Of course I was on the wrong page. I turned to the "Introduction" page and kept my eyes glued on her.

"The War Between the States was the bloodiest war in United States history. Many stories, half truths, and distorted facts were told by both the Union and the Confederates. Today, historians are still arguing and researching which of these stories are true and which ones were created by clever people's imaginations.

"For the next four weeks we're going to discuss these stories and half-truths. I'm dividing the class into pairs. Each pair will find a story and try to determine if the story is true or made up. Select your partners and let's begin."

I waited while the rest of the class picked and chose their partners. It was no surprise when Pit Bull chose Lola Simms, nor when Wendy tapped Roberto on the arm and asked. Raul ignored me as if I didn't exist. I saw him get up and walk towards Christine. She sat on the edge of her chair, her hands clasped in her lap.

Ms. Yolanda watched me. I felt her eyes single me out. She tapped her nails against the podium, a rhythmic beat that stuck in my brain. I glanced around the auditorium. Most of the class had paired off with their friends. All the groups stayed within their pecking order. The black kids paired with the black kids. The adventurers paired with the charity whites. The Hispanics turned towards the Asians.

I was the only one left without a partner. Ms. Yolanda stepped away from the podium and walked to the edge of the stairwell. I saw her step down and pause. Raul stood alone. I guess Catherine didn't want Burrito Boy as her partner and she chose Joseph Wang instead.

Ms. Yolanda waved at Raul and then pointed her finger at me. Raul looked down at his feet.

"Raul," Ms. Yolanda said.

That's all I heard. Raul stepped forward. He placed one foot in front of the other, and then gained momentum as he strolled towards me.

"Thanks," I said.

"I guess we're in this together."

He shrugged.

"I was on my way to ask Ms. Yolanda if I could do it alone, but…"

Raul spread his arms apart.

"It might as well be you."

I didn't know what to say. I wanted to take his hand and hold it, but it would look dumb, so I just muttered, "I appreciate it."

"You'd better."

Ms. Yolanda stepped up onto the stage and walked back to the podium. She faced the class. "Now that you've chosen, discuss what myth or legend you want to do. In pairs, come up to the stage and tell me so I can write it down. There are plenty to choose from so there shouldn't be any duplicates."

Raul and I caught each other's eyes and grinned. We climbed the steps leading to the stage and approached Ms. Yolanda.

"You know your topic?" Ms. Yolanda asked us, her pen poised.

"Yes, Ma'am," Raul said. "Anna Mae and I want to investigate the lost Confederate gold of Jefferson Davis."

"That's been a mystery for over a hundred forty years since Davis fled Richmond, Virginia. It's a puzzler."

"It sure is," I said.

Ms. Yolanda wrote, "The Lost Confederate Gold of Jefferson Davis" in her notebook. "Two written reports, an oral presentation and an outline, please, and make it unique."

"No problem," Raul said, dragging me away from the podium.

Pit Bull and Lola waited until Raul and I left the stage. They stepped up the stairs and swaggered towards Ms. Yolanda. I heard Lola say, "Our topic is on whether Abraham Lincoln saw his own death in a dream before John Wilkes Booth shot him at Ford Theatre."

Ms. Yolanda sighed. "Are you sure, Lola, Stanley, that you can do this?"

I never heard their answer. I was no longer physically standing in the auditorium next to Raul. I was driving a wagon, following a regiment of Rebel soldiers.

The wagon jolted over the pot-holed dirt road. Sitting on a wooden seat with my legs tucked underneath me, my joints ached. Sitting next to me was a black Confederate soldier. Surrounding the wagon, cries from the infantry pierced my ears. I drove a wagon with a two-mule team.

We'd just pulled into the front yard of Chennault Plantation. I ached all over. We'd been traveling since before dawn. My shoulders and hands were stiff, raw and bleeding.

The rough-hewn seat hurt my rear. I shifted my weight. My left leg cramped. My wagonmate stared at my bulging leg muscle. He leaned down and massaged it with his long, slender fingers. His rifle lay across his lap.

A whippoorwill cried out to its mate. I sniffed the air. A mixture of wood smoke and rotten meat filled my nostrils. My lips quivered. My wagonmate put his forefinger to his lips. "Shh, I hear somethin'."

I strained my ears. My wagonmate pointed with his rifle. I followed its barrel. A brown-haired man, dressed in civilian clothing, crawled out from behind the shrubs that bordered the house's front porch, about a hundred yards away from us. He straightened and strode towards us. Both of his hands were stretched out.

A bullet whined overhead. The man froze, and then ran blindly, stumbling over small bushes in his haste to get away.

My wagonmate stood, twisted, and aimed his rifle at someone behind us. In slow motion, he squeezed the trigger. The rifle kicked, but my wagonmate held his footing.

I heard shouts. Panicked, I dove off the seat and flattened myself under the wagon, holding my breath. Above me, my wagonmate continued shooting. I heard the chamber click as he reloaded several times. He stopped shooting after several moments, then climbed down. He held out his hand. "You kin git up now. Whoever wuz shootin' stopped. Captain says we're to git out."

"Wha' 'bout the wagons?"

"Leave 'em 'ere. We've done wha' we kin. No sense in gettin' kilt. Take wha' you kin carry, Captain says. We'll bury our share and come back fer it later."

I grabbed the wagon's side and hauled myself up. My wagonmate's face blurred. His skin seemed to merge with Raul's black skin. His face swam into sight. "Anna Mae!" I heard him call out, "Are you okay?"

I blinked and noticed that I was back in the auditorium. For the first time, I noticed that Raul had liquid brown eyes. His hand clasped my shoulder. I took a deep breath and shook my head. It had seemed so real.

Blue high-heeled pumps soon joined his sneakers. I glanced up. Ms. Yolanda stood three inches away from me. Her green eyes met my brown ones. "You had me worried, Anna Mae. Are you okay?"

I scrambled to my feet and looked about. There was no sign of a wagon, mules or two black Confederate soldiers. Pit Bull, Lola, Catherine, and the rest of the class stood behind Ms. Yolanda. I saw them exchange puzzled glances. They shook their heads in unison, like so many puppets.

I decided to play dumb. "What happened?"

Raul's lips parted, "You sat on the floor, pointing your finger towards Ms. Yolanda. Five seconds later, you leaned over and flattened yourself on the floor underneath the overhang of the stage."

"I did that?"

Christine grabbed Raul's arm and pulled him away from me. I sucked in my breath. Ms. Yolanda grasped my shoulders and turned me around to face her. She knelt on one knee. "You'd better sit down. Catherine, get her a glass of water from the teacher's lounge. Ask one of teachers to get it for you. Tell them Ms. Yolanda sent you. That's all you need to say."

Catherine walked out of the room. Raul went back to his seat, rubbing his arm. Ms. Yolanda waved the rest of the class back to their seats. Five minutes later, Catherine returned with a glass of water. She handed it to Ms. Yolanda, who gave it to me. Catherine sat next to me, holding one of my hands. Her hands were cool and soothed my hot flesh.

Ms. Yolanda watched as I drank one sip of water at a time. Her eyes never left my face. I could tell she was worried, but didn't want to say so.

"I'll let you be, but be more careful in the future." She walked away and mounted the steps that led up to the stage.

Catherine took the glass from me when I was finished. She dropped my hand and started to walk out. At the doorway, Ms. Yolanda called out after her, "I'll take the glass."

Catherine sighed and turned towards the steps. She climbed them and gave Ms. Yolanda the empty glass.

Raul sat in the chair that Catherine had vacated.

"What did you see this time?"

"I thought you were mad at me."

"I'm not sure what to think. Pit Bull and Lola don't count, but the rest of the class thinks you've got a loose noodle. After seeing that black fist, flying chalk and eraser, who am I to say? 'Sides, when I saw your eyes, I wasn't sure you were you or if you were someone else."

"What's that supposed to mean?"

Raul searched my face with his gaze. "You didn't act like you were twelve years old, girl. You acted like a boy, all grown up. For all I know, someone else had taken over your body completely."

This time I stared directly into his eyes. We held each other's stare for five seconds, and then he broke contact. I lowered mine and reached down, without thinking, and rubbed my left leg. It ached. Raul's eyes followed my hand massage.

"What's wrong with your leg?"

"Cramps! My toes are numb too."

"When did this start?"

I stopped rubbing my leg and wriggled my toes. The burning sensation stopped. "It's like I've been sitting for hours and my toes went to sleep."

Raul sighed. Ms. Yolanda looked at us. The whole class looked at us. One by one, each kid lifted their hand and put it to the side of their head. They extended two fingers and twirled them in a circle. My stomach twisted and turned upside down. I was a marked kid.

I heard a shrill noise and looked up. Above me, hanging in mid-air, was the black fist. It imitated the class's actions and pointed its forefinger down at me.

Chapter Five

I kept to myself after that display. When a phantom ghost mocked me, I knew the rest of the real world was against me. Raul kept to himself and read the whole "Myths and Legend" chapter without sharing one thought with me. Tears burned my eyes. I sneaked a tissue out of my backpack and tried not to sob out loud. Anyone else I could've shut out, but seeing Raul sit straight and stiff besides me was too much.

Hunching down in my seat, I read through tear-dropped eyes. I sniffed once or twice to get Raul's attention. It didn't work. He half turned in his seat. I could tell that Raul hated me. Miserable, I watched the second hand on my watch tick off the seconds until the final bell of the day rang. Twenty minutes later, it did.

Sighing, I picked up my backpack from the floor and marched towards the door. I kept my eyes down. Reaching the door, I waited for Pit Bull, Lola, and their gang to walk out first. It wasn't a good idea to leave before your betters.

Raul shuffled out with Catherine and Wendy hanging on to each of his arms. I watched him through slit eyes.

They pushed their way by me. No "excuse me" or "sorry," the three of them just waltzed by me.

I soon caught up with Raul. By then, Catherine and Wendy said their good-byes and walked off arm in arm. They lived in a different section of town, and waited for the city bus to come and pick them up. Raul glanced at me, and then shifted his gaze.

"Nice of you to join me," he said.

I sauntered up to him and walked by in rigid silence. Pretending I was the one hurt by his behavior, I ignored his comment.

"Fine, have it your way."

"Did you say somethin'?" I asked.

He pressed his thin lips together. My face burned hot. I needed friends beyond my brother, Malcolm. I stared down at my sneakers.

"Okay, here goes," I muttered. "I'm sorry. I ran without thinking. It scared me. It won't happen again. Stick a needle in my eye if I say this as a lie."

Raul hefted his backpack and started walking forwards. I lunged and grabbed his left arm.

"I...I got spooked."

Raul pried my fingers from his arm and flung my hand off. He doubled his pace.

"All right!" I screeched.

I threw my backpack on the ground in front of him

"Have it your way. Don' 'spect me t' come ovah t'night and 'splain tha' fist to yar abuelito and abuelita. Go rot in hell!"

That did it. Raul turned and took two giant steps backwards until his nose touched mine. He grabbed both of my shoulders and shook me, then he pulled me in till his lips touched mine.

"Listen, Anna Mae, yar the one who betrayed me, not the other way around. Don't blame me. Ya ran out durin' a fire drill and left me in the dust. I could've burnt to a crisp."

"Ya wouldn't, I s'pose. Don' play hero with me, Raul. I wasn't the only one runnin'. Pit Bull, Lola, all of them adventurers, charities, blacks, and wongs ran like hell to get out first. Yar precious friend Christine trod on the heels of my sneakers. I still have the marks. Wanna see?"

I bent over and turned my sweat socks outward. Black smudge marks dirtied the outside surface. Raul leaned down. He reached out and peeled down one of my socks and studied my ankle. A small purple bruise appeared on the back of it. He slid the sock up my calf. I snatched my foot away.

He picked up my backpack and handed it to me. He filled his cheeks with air and sighed.

"You pissed me off when you ran off."

"Do ya still want me t' come ovah t'night?"

"Are ya crazy? Of course I do! I can't face them alone! I need all the help I can get. Trust me. 'Sides, Abuelito is funny 'bout stuff like that. He doesn' believe in ghosts. Thinks it's a pack of nonsense. Abuelita, she's got two kinds of faith—one spiritual and the other..."

Raul shrugged.

"Let's just say Abuelita goes to church every Sunday morning and stays until late in the day. She comes home, fixes supper, and we eat late, with lots of candlelight."

"Sounds 'bout right. Poppa and Momma tell me they don' believe in God. As for Granma Zora, I'm not sure wha' she's into. Hard t' know wha' she thinks."

Raul frowned, his puckered lips drooping downwards

"Abuelito once told me to stay 'way from two subjects: politics and religion. Guess there's a reason for it."

"The same reason we held our sixth grade prom in the cafeteria and the whites held theirs in the gym last year."

"Can't change the way things are. Been this way for as long as I've lived here, and you too. Folks are just like that. You know that."

"Don' have to like it."

"Didn't say you have to."

Raul shrugged, glanced down the tracks and sighed. "See anythin' comin'?"

"Nope. I like lookin' down them though. It's a road outta here."

"Nevah thought 'bout it much."

I stared down the tracks. As far as my eye could see, the tracks stretched onwards and disappeared into horizon. For a moment, I wished that I could follow those tracks and leave Lowry, Georgia and its contradictions far behind me. Raul tugged at my bare arm. He shifted his backpack.

"Gotta go. I promised them I'd be home at 3:30 cuz of company."

"Company, huh? I've been promoted. When will ya abuelita call?"

"Right away. Good 'nough?"

I nodded and ran the rest of the way home. Malcolm met me at the door. He opened it before I took out my key and inserted it into the lock.

"Where's Granma?"

My voice echoed in the hallway. Malcolm shrugged. "Food shoppin'."

He shifted his weight from one foot to the other. Malcolm shuddered. He rolled his eyes.

"I'm glad you're here. It's too quiet."

"Too quiet?"

I sniffed the air and wished I hadn't. A terrible, horrible smell permeated the room. "Malcolm, did you just fart? Ugh!" I gagged.

Malcolm took a deep breath. He clutched his stomach. "I don't feel too good."

I took a cautious sniff. The odor came from the kitchen. I put my backpack down on the floor. Step by step I walked down the hallway and pushed the kitchen door inwards.

I squeezed my nose. My eyes watered. On the counters two large rats were chasing each other, their sharp claws scratching the countertops. Their black eyes raked me. Bits of garbage littered the floor. Carrot peelings, limp lettuce leaves, leftover baked beans, a two-day old plastic milk carton and scattered shredded paper towels covered the floor and countertop. One rat jumped from the counter and ran towards us. I shoved Malcolm backwards. "Get outta here!"

Malcolm stood and stared. The second rat pounced to the floor and scurried towards him. That broke him. Malcolm rushed to the kitchen table and leaped. He stood on the tabletop, lifting his legs, squeezing his hands and yelling, "Shoo! Shoo!"

Frantic, I dashed to the utility closet and grabbed the broom. Holding it over my head, I ran back and struck at the first rat. I missed it. The second one scampered towards the half-open cupboard door. I raised the broom and brought it down hard. The rat squealed. Behind me, I heard something plop inside the sink. Nails scratched against the porcelain. Click. Click. Click.

"Flush 'em!" I yelled at Malcolm. Water splashed into the sink and hit me.

"Thanks!"

That's when I saw Malcolm jump from the table. He landed two feet away from me and seized the broom.

"Turn off the water," he yelled.

I turned and watched. The rat lay still in the sink full

of hot water. I saw the steam rise from the liquid surface. Puzzled, I turned and faced Malcolm.

"How dija do it so fast?"

"What do ya mean?"

"You drowned the othahh rat."

"No, I didn'. I was on the table, too scared to move. You must've done it yo'self without thinkin' 'bout it."

"Is it dead?"

I peered at the broom. It still rested on top of the second rat. Malcolm lifted the broomstick. The straw bristles bent in all directions. The rat lay motionless on the kitchen floor. I picked up the stainless steel garbage can lid and banged it on top of the rat.

"I think it's dead," Malcolm said.

"Hope so."

I gagged and stumbled towards the sink. I threw up and stared into the vile water. The rat floated to the surface. Malcolm joined me and looked at the mess.

"Ugh, yo goin' to clean it up 'fore Granma gets back?"

"Clean wha' up?" A deep guttural voice drawled.

A strong breeze whipped through the kitchen. Paper napkins, plastic cups, tablemats and shredded paper towel bits blew away. A Caucasian man stomped through the kitchen, dressed in a blood-stained blue uniform. His gray eyes bulged. His chest heaved. I saw the medals pinned to his chest move up and down. His face twisted to one side, leaving his lips at odds with each other. His mouth looked like an "x." He lifted his dirty hands to his waist and stared.

With his feet spread apart he gasped one word—"Water."

Malcolm reached up into the cabinet and took out a tumbler. He turned on the faucet and filled it with clean water. The ghost reached out with his dirty hand and grasped the tumbler. He brought it up to his bloodless lips and drank it all down in three gulps.

"More!"

Malcolm grabbed the tumbler and put it under the faucet. He turned the water on and filled the glass a second time. This time the ghost leaned forward and took the glass. He threw the water into his face. It dripped from his skin and down the front of his blue gold-buttoned uniform, and yet I never saw the tunic jacket get wet. The water puddled on it, but it didn't soak in. That didn't make any sense.

I stared until my eyeballs stung. The water didn't drip down to the floor either. How queer was that?

The ghost didn't pay any attention except to his thirst. He kept gulping the water down. His Adam's apple bobbed up and down in his throat. It gave me the creeps. Malcolm edged closer to me until his hand touched mine.

Like the fist the first morning, I felt compelled to look for answers.

"Who are you?"

The ghost turned its sightless eyes towards me. "I'm a Union soldier."

That bit of information didn't help me at all. I knew about slavery and Southern plantation owners. I knew about Abraham Lincoln and his Emancipation Proclamation that freed the slaves, but ... I found this ghost curious. It saw Malcolm and me, even though it had no eyes. It spoke, even though its mouth was blown away.

"Have you seen any darkies?" The ghost asked.

Malcolm's grip on my hand tightened.

"No, I haven't," I croaked.

The kitchen grew colder. The windows frosted. On the floor, the garbage can lid was coated with a thin layer of ice. I shoved Malcolm in front of me.

"It's time to leave," I said, my voice rising.

Malcolm froze. I pushed him about an inch closer to the door.

"Get movin'! I'm not kiddin'!" I whispered.

The ghost rose into the air and floated towards us. I kept shoving Malcolm until he was halfway to the door. He woke up and crept forward. I heard his teeth chatter.

"Go!"

This time Malcolm high-tailed it out of the kitchen. He never looked back. I followed and we ran down the hallway, until we got to the staircase. Taking two steps at a time, we rushed up the steps. On the landing, we looked down the steps. The ghost had followed us. It hovered in mid-air like a gigantic inflated balloon. Its giant black boots hovered in the air, with overlarge silver spurs. They clanged as the ghost charged towards us.

I dragged Malcolm from the landing and into his room. Barricading the door with his desk chair, I pushed his bed against the chair and piled both with books and toys. Not satisfied, I threw him into his clothes closet and followed Malcolm in and slammed the door shut.

We listened and waited. We heard no booted feet climbing the stairs after us. I held my breath and willed my pounding heart to slow down. I looked at Malcolm. He had curled up into a ball. I saw his eyes blink. His arms were crossed tight against his chest.

I counted the seconds. They turned into minutes. I froze. Outside the door, I heard a familiar voice.

"Malcolm? Anna Mae?"

"Granma!" Malcolm whimpered. "Let go of me!"

Malcolm uncurled and clambered to his feet. He kicked the closet door open and dashed out. I heard books and toys strike the floor. The bed squealed as Malcolm pushed it away from the door. I saw the chair slide across the floor. The door crashed open as it hit the wall.

"Granma!" Malcolm shouted.

I crawled out of the closet and got to my feet. Stiff legged, I closed the closet door. I felt stupid.

Granma Zora, with Malcolm clasped in her arms, stood in the hallway.

"Wha' were y'all doin'? Dead rat in the sink. Garbage can lid in the middle of the kitchen floor. Land sakes almighty, it's 'nough t' scare a body," Granma said.

I looked down at my flip-flops. How could I answer her without sounding dumb? "Two rats got into the house. Malcolm killed one with the broom. The other one drowned somehow."

Granma hugged Malcolm for being Malcolm. I waited for my hug, but it never came. *Figures! Granma always did take Malcolm's side.*

"Guess the rats were attracted to the garbage can. Forgot to empty it this morning before school. Won't happen again. Sorry."

Granma thawed a bit. "Why were yo' hidin' in Malcolm's closet? I heard his bed bein' shoved 'way from the door. Who were yo' protectin' Malcolm from? A haint?"

She waited for my answer. Malcolm pried himself loose from Granma and stood with his left arm straddling her shoulders.

"We were playin' hide-and-seek. I guess we got carried away," I crossed my fingers behind my back. I knew that Malcolm saw what I did with my hands. I hoped Granma Zora didn't see. Momma would say it was a sign of guilt.

"All right. Go 'long with yo' and clean up tha' mess. Time for supper in a bit."

I sighed and slapped Malcolm's arm. Granma pulled him into her arms a second time and gave him another hug. I marched downstairs and got rid of the two rats. One I wrapped up in some old newspaper that I got from the shed. The other one I used one of Granma's rubber gloves and lifted it out of the gross water. I threw both rats into the outdoor garbage can. I banged the lid on and placed a rock on top of it so it wouldn't fall off.

Next I took the mop from the utility closet and rinsed the rat's blood from the floor. Taking a green plastic trash bag from the utility shelf, I picked up the food scraps and the other garbage and dumped them into the trashcan. I washed the rest of the kitchen with hydrogen peroxide and hot water. As I worked, I heard someone whistle "Dixie." I turned my head. My eyes darted around the kitchen, but I couldn't see anyone—or anything.

Chapter Six

The phone rang.

"I'll get it!" I yelled out.

Dropping the mop, I dashed to the phone and picked it up on the second ring. Granma arrived in the kitchen, huffing and puffing. She stood with her hand stretched out. I gave her the receiver. With drooped shoulders, I trudged to the mop and picked it up. I finished swabbing the floor and stowed the wet mop upright in the utility closet.

Flouncing over to the dinette chair, I sat down. I rested my head on upturned fists. I stared at the damp floor. Granma spoke into the receiver.

"This is Zora Kingsley. Juanita? Nice t'hear from yo'. Anna Mae? Supper? T'night?"

I waited, drumming my fingertips on the tabletop. Granma stopped talking. I looked up. She turned to face me, her eyes a huge question mark.

"Yo' wanna go ovah to Raul's t'night for supper?"

I nodded my head up and down. "I guess tha's okay. Be sure she's home by 8:30. It's a school night. Nice talkin' t' yo', too."

71

Granma put the phone down and glanced at me. "Wha's up?"

I dropped my eyes. I drew lines and circles on the table with my fingertips.

"It's a school night, chile, and Juanita wanted yo' ovah. Somthin' yo' friend ain't tellin'?

"Sorta like tha'."

I kept my eyes focused on the table. Granma walked off, humming. I breathed a sigh of relief. The kitchen door swung open. The odor of Poppa's aftershave hit my nose. I quivered.

"Malcolm, you didn't."

"Yo' smell nice," Granma said.

The doorbell chimed. I got up from the chair and shoved the door out of my way. I ran down the hallway and threw open the front door. Raul stood on the porch, wearing his favorite patched blue cut-off jeans and an olive drab t-shirt. He wore thick-sole sandals on his feet.

"Who is it, chile?"

Granma's voice thundered down the hallway. Malcolm galloped through the kitchen door.

"Hiya, Raul."

Malcolm beamed. Raul stepped back and waved his hand in front of his nose.

"Yo' like?" Malcolm said. "It's Poppa's. Thought I woul' try it out."

Raul coughed.

"It's uh nice, real nice. You ready?"

"Bye Granma. Latah squirt," I said.

Granma barreled through the door. She held out her sweater.

"Gets cool in the evenin's. Bettah take this with you. I 'pect yo' home by 8:30 and not a minute latah. 'Kay?"

"Bye, granma. See ya, Malcolm."

I stood on the front porch and sighed. The door closed behind us.

"Let's split 'fore Malcolm thinks of somethin' else."

I ran down the steps and out into the road.

"Meet yo' at the railroad tracks," I called over my shoulder.

We reached the tracks at the same time. Even in sandals, Raul ran fast. Breathless, we trudged the rest of the way towards his grandparent's trailer. Raul's house was different from the rest of the houses in Lowry.

Raul's was two stories tall. The second floor had a tilt-up roof which enclosed the second story living space. Its roof had hinging rafters just above Raul's bedroom. Raul told me that the walls folded up which gave him extra floor space because the floor extended up under the eaves. The windows were special because they were in the shape of an E thus reducing the heat that penetrated most clapboard's thin walls.

Both stories of the trailer sported white paint. The roof was painted red and sloped. His Abuelita planted bushes in front. In the middle of the yard an angel statue stood. Water flowed from its mouth while a cement cherub played his silent harp. White and red pebbles covered the front yard. Two donkey statues carried two young boys wearing sombreros. His Abuelito's old white Cadillac sat in the crumbling concrete driveway.

Raul's Abuelito opened the front door. He was a thin man with a slight paunch to his stomach. He wore a white collarless shirt. The shirt was double hemmed and hung halfway over his black pants. His Abuelito wore a red sash around his waist instead of a leather belt. A trimmed mustache set off his squared lips and long oval face. "Welcome to our house, Anna Mae. I'm pleased to meet you. Your Granma called and insisted you be home by eight thirty."

My face warmed. I laughed, embarrassed that granma made such a big deal out of it. Raul pulled me into his house before I had a melt down. Abuelito closed the door and followed behind us.

Raul led me into the kitchen. It was a lot bigger than I remembered. Abuelita was the exact opposite of her husband. She was solid and compact. She wore a white blouse, embroidered with red, yellow, and orange flowers with green tangled weeds and small insects crawling, inching, and flying on her skirt's hem. Abuelita stepped away from the oven and shook my hand. "Welcome! It's nice to finally meet you. Raul speaks about you constantly. Anna Mae said this. Anna Mae said that. I feel that we know you already. Supper will be ready in twenty minutes. Raul, take Anna Mae upstairs and show her your room. Abuelito will call you when supper is on the table."

I curtseyed, then muttered, "Nice meeting y'all," and retreated.

Raul dragged me out of the kitchen. I heard them laughing whether it was aimed at me or not, I didn't know. The curtsey must've done the trick. I stole a look at Raul's face. He smiled. For now, I was out of the dog house with him. I sighed and looked about me. Raul took me through the dining room and back into a short lavender painted hallway. I saw a circular stairwell that led up to the second floor in the middle of the room. "Neat, huh?" Abuelita told me she always wanted a circular staircase. Don't ask my why. I've stopped trying to figure out my grandparents a long time ago.

He stepped on the first metal mesh stair. Taking two steps at a time, Raul got to the solid wood landing before I did. I was too busy staring at the pictures on the walls.

A variety of pictures hung. Two of them were sea scenes: fishing boats, drying nets, and racks of fish. The others consisted of group portraits, old gnarled men, heavy-set women and overdressed children. One child reminded me of Raul, but I wasn't sure. The boy had puckered cheeks with black eyes narrowed to slits.

The walls of the house were painted a pale rose shade and color coordinated with the bluish purple wall painted on the upstairs wall. When I reached the second floor, I noticed that the floors were wood. Good sliding potential with socks, I thought and wondered if Raul ever tried doing that.

I looked down the hallway. No sign of Raul. I inched my way down the passage looking into opened bedroom doors. I saw white bedspreads and plastic wrapped lampshades.

Raul called out.

"I'm in here,"

His voice came from further down the hallway. I skipped towards the end of the corridor and peered in to the last room on the left. An open door led into his bedroom. I strode in. A Paper Mache donkey piñata greeted me. It dangled from a black cord hanging from a planter's hook in the middle of the ceiling. Baseballs, baseball cards, bats, mitts, and balls rested on two dressers, a bed chest and a desk. A replica of the Enterprise spaceship dangled over his bed. Books and comics lined bookshelves set into the wall. An old freight trunk took up the remainder of the wall. Stray socks and shirts stuck out of drawers half pushed in.

On the opposite wall, a row of hooks stuck out. A denim jacket, yellow slicker, a torn sweater, and a navy blue sweatshirt with the Atlanta Braves tag still on it hung from the hooks. Raul was bouncing on his bed when I walked in. He threw his pillow at me and stopped bouncing. We stared at each other. Outside of Malcolm's bedroom, I never found myself in a boy's bedroom before.

"Now wha'?" I said.

He snapped his fingers.

"I know, let's play a game." Raul laid down on his stomach. He reached under his bed. I heard him pushing stuff aside. "Aha, got it!" he said.

Raul pulled out a cardboard box and swiped the dust off of the box cover with his bare arm.

"This ought to keep us out of trouble."

Raul smiled. "It's a game of strategy and mystery. Whoever finds success as a particular person wins. You on?"

"What kind of game is that?"

Raul shrugged. "Of choices."

I watched as Raul removed the cover. He took out 20 game pieces. Each one he righted and placed on the floor. He laid the written instructions on the floor in front of me. "It's called *Life Choices*. The object of the game is to become a famous historical person by making the right choices. The winner is the one who succeeds at becoming that person without violating the rules, principals, and laws outlined in the instructions."

"It's different. I'll give yo' that. Who gave yo' this game?"

"A friend of Abuelito. He says his kids play it all the time. It keeps them out of his hair."

"It figures. Okay, what's next."

He set up the board. Next, he removed about 20 games pieces painted different colors: black, brown, yellow, white, and red. A set of cards followed. He placed them in the middle of the board. Raul handed me the instructions. I looked at them and groaned.

"Do we have to read this?"

"Naw, let's take the easy way. We start here."

I glanced at the board. The word "GO" glared up at me.

"What's next?"

"I spin. Here, take this piece."

Raul handed me a black woman with a yellow parasol painted in her outstretched hand. He took a brown piece that looked like a soldier dressed in a 20th century uniform.

"Now what?"

Raul spun the dial. It stopped. He advanced his soldier into the first country. It was marked Africa. I shrugged. Something caught my eye. My woman, it moved by itself. I held my breath. Raul stopped talking and froze.

"Didja move that?"

I locked gazes with him.

"Would it make yo feel bettah if I say yes?"

He shook his head. We both watched the board. His bedroom grew cooler. I saw his breath. I grabbed his hand.

"R-a-u-l," my voice drew out his name in separate letters.

Raul gripped my fingers. We scrambled to our feet. The pieces crept on the board. The spinner spun in rapid succession. Voices. Harsh laughter. The smell of burned wood and boiled coffee. Pop! Pop! Pop! The Piñata swayed back and forth. His bedroom door swung shut.

"Raul," I said again.

We found ourselves by the half opened door. Raul squeezed through and dragged me along. The door banged shut. We fled down the hallway and galloped down the stairs. At the bottom of the stairwell, Raul and I tilted our heads. Footsteps thudded on the ceiling.

Abuelito stood in the entrance to the living room and waved to us.

"Supper is ready."

Chapter Seven

Raul crossed into the dining room. I stopped short. A white, embroidered, flowered tablecloth graced the table. Bright orange and yellow plates, water glasses and cloth napkins lay on it. Abuelito pulled out my chair and waited until I was seated. Raul sat on the opposite side of the table. His grandparents also sat at opposite ends. In the center stood a large silver bowl of red and pink carnations surrounded by green ferns. The entire table looked festive.

Abuelita came out of the kitchen carrying a large white ceramic bowl. Steam rose from it. "We'll start with Raul's favorite, homemade alphabet noodle soup."

Raul frowned. I giggled happy that I wasn't the only kid embarrassed by their granma. I felt right at home.

Abuelito laughed. "That one, he doesn't have any brothers or sisters to tease him, so Mamma and I do it to keep him humble."

Abuelita set the bowl down in front of her husband. She handed him the ladle. He took the first soup bowl and filled it half way. I watched as he ladled the soup into each of the three bowls. Raul slouched in his chair pouting. I ignored him and watched his grandparents, instead. When Abuelito finished dishing the soup out, Abuelita sat down. She extended her hand and clasped mine. Abuelito reached for my left hand and grabbed Raul's right hand. We formed a prayer circle.

We all bowed our heads. One minute of silence passed. Abuelito lifted his head first and dropped my hand. "We can eat."

Raul picked up his soup spoon and dipped it into his bowl. I took my napkin, unfolded it, and spread it over my lap. I picked up my spoon and paused. The noodle alphabet letters formed a word on the liquid surface. I stared and squirmed. I glanced at Abuelito. He sat poised with his spoon frozen half way between his bowl and lips. I swiveled my eyes toward Abuelita. She sat rigid; her napkin held tight in her fingers.

I swung my gaze to Raul. His eyes were enormous. "Raul!" I hissed. "Look inside my soup bowl."

Raul stood up, leaned over the table and peered into my bowl.

"Wha' do yo' see?"

My soup rippled like a breeze ruffling water. A cold breath hissed across my face. The letters split apart. New letters formed a word. I saw Raul's lips twitch.

"*FRENCH GOLD!*"

"Wha' does tha' mean, French Gold?" Raul asked.

My voice rose. "Yar askin' me? Get the soup t' tell yo'"

We both fixated on the letters. They split and then regrouped. I watched as the noodle letters rose to the surface. The discarded ones sank to the bottom of the bowl. I felt Raul's cold breath on my nose. His eyes lined up with mine. We both watched and waited. A second phrase appeared. "*BURIED COINS.*"

Other words appeared, and then broke apart as we read each one aloud. "*FEDERAL TROOPS!*" "*ASK*

MARYANNE!" "*WARTHEN'S, GA!*" "*BOMFORD GOLD*" Raul fell back into his seat. He covered his eyes with both hands.

"Didja do that?"

"I, I'm not sure."

Raul took his hands away from his eyes. His eyes twitched. He glanced down into my soup bowl. The noodle letters sank out of sight. They no longer spelled any words. "Does this happen when yo' visit yar othahh friends?" His voice squeaked out.

"No, nevah."

Raul pushed his chair away from the table and got to his feet. I left the table as well. My napkin fell to the floor. "Where are yo' goin?"

"Don' know. Don' care. Yar spookin' me again. I don' like it."

"What time is it?"

Raul checked his watch. "Six thirty, we've got time."

I peeked at his grandparents. "They're still out of it. Jus like Ms. Yolanda and Principal Teddy. Wondah why?"

"Cuz their adults, not kids. Adults don' believe in ghosts most of the time."

"My granma does," I said.

Raul says, "She does?"

I said, "Sometimes."

Raul stopped talking. A splash of liquid hit the tablecloth. He crept back to the table, leaned on both hands and stared at my bowl. Its surface pitched as if a breeze caught the liquid and disturbed it. Raul picked up a spoon and stirred. Chunks of chicken, carrots, and alphabet noodles boiled to the surface. "Nothing ever happened like this before."

I shrugged and looked at the soup.

"It looks like soup...now."

Abuelita eyes darted from me to Raul, and then to Abuelito.

"How do you like your soup, Anna Mae?"

"It's delicious." I said not knowing what else to say. How do you explain the unexplainable?

When we finished eating the soup, Abuelita asked me if I wanted more. I declined, but Raul nodded yes. Abuelita ladled a second helping into his bowl. Abuelito excused himself and cleared the soup bowls off the table. Raul continued eating. Nothing happened this time. We exchanged glances. No breezes. No cold spots. The noodles remained noodles. I sighed, and waited for the meat course.

Abuelito returned to the table carrying a tray of goodies. Raul named each one in Spanish as he pointed them out to me. "This is Picudillo. It's served over white rice. We use black rice. I like it better than brown rice. It's got ground beef, potatoes, onions, green peppers and tomatoes in it. Abuelita serves it with sangria; it's a sweet wine with oranges, lemons, and lime slices. They drink that. We drink homemade lemonade."

Once we finished eating the Picudillo, Abuelita left the table. I got up and cleared the table. I glared at Raul, but he just sat back and grinned. I returned from the kitchen empty handed and sat down.

"What's for dessert?"

"Wait and see," Raul said.

Abuelita entered the dining room. Abuelito held the door opened with his foot. In his hand, he held a plate of puffed pastry. The tray that Abuelita held was full of decorative sweet breads. Walnuts and dried fruit stuck out of it.

She placed the tray on the table the same time that Abuelito did. He disappeared back into the kitchen and returned with a plastic shaped Teddy bear filled with an amber liquid. Abuelito placed the honey bear on the table with a plastic spoon. "Ready for dessert?"

Raul smacked his lips and reached out with both hands. I watched as Raul selected a pastry and took a slice of fruit bread. He broke the bread in half. A long thin piece of white paper unfurled. I stared until my eyes blurred. In slow motion, Raul picked up the paper scrap. His lips moved, but I heard nothing.

In a fog, I reached my hand across the table and grasped the scrap from Raul's hand. *Anna Mae Botts, beware of flames.* The paper crackled as I crumpled it. I saw his grandparent's faces. They raised their eyes and stared at me as if I had sprouted horns and wings. Raul reached for his water glass. It tipped over and spilled. The water splashed me. I jumped from my chair and knocked the chair over. Water soaked the tablecloth and my shorts.

No one spoke or did they? Their lips moved. They gesticulated with their hands. Yet, I still couldn't hear a word they said. My body trembled. I couldn't stop shaking. My pigtails flopped across my face as my head moved back and forth.

Raul's face popped into view. He parted my pigtails. Abuelito stood next to me. He grasped my arm. The room spun. Raul's grandfather had four eyes. My head ached. My heart thumped. Daylight narrowed to a thin point. I strained, trying to see, and then there was only blackness.

Chapter Eight

A figure shot through the narrowed opening. She held out her arms and enclosed me in a tight embrace. "Call me Protectora, daughter of Exu. I am here within you."

"Anna Mae?"

Raul called me. I heard his voice, thin. It quavered like it came from an old man. Strong, tight fingers dug deep into both my shoulders.

"Stop shaking me!"

All swirled around me in confusion. Raul led me to the chair. I sat down. Their cleared table bothered me. I didn't remember it being cleared. I looked up into Abuelita's face. Her lips said one thing. Her eyes said another.

"Why don't you and Raul go upstairs. We'll call you when we're finished tidying up the kitchen."

Raul steadied me. We left the table together and headed for the living room. Neither one of us wanted to go back upstairs, not yet.

"It takes them forever to wash and dry the dishes."

"Really?"

I tried sitting still on the sofa, but couldn't. The Protectora kept getting in the way so I stood. I wanted to ask Raul about her, but something held me back. I paced back and forth as I waited for Raul's grandparents.

"You okay?" Raul said.

"Yeah, sure, peachy."

"You fainted back there."

"That's not all that happened," I finally said.

Raul stepped up to me. He forced his face into mine. "What happened?"

I tried saying Protectora, but my tongue refused to move. "Where's your bathroom?"

Raul pointed back towards the hallway. "Second door on the right under the stairwell. Yo' can't miss it."

I hurried to the bathroom. I opened the door and quickly squeezed it shut behind me. The face in the mirror wasn't smiling. It wasn't my reflection. I turned on the faucet. Water blasted the sink. Cupping my hands, I thrust them under the faucet and collected a fist full of water. I threw the water into my face. It felt cool, comforting.

The hand towel landed in my hands. "Thanks," I muttered and realized that the towel flew into my hands. I grabbed the doorknob and twisted. The door flew opened. I dashed out and ran into the living room. Raul and his grandparents looked up.

Abuelito and Abuelita sat on the sofa facing Raul. He stood in front of the fireplace set in the middle of the room. Raul stood there bouncing from foot to foot.

"Wondered what was taking so long."

"I'm here, now. Let's get this over with," I said.

I felt like someone else stood by me. Their hot breath washing over me, I ignored it as best I could.

"Anna Mae, you know why Raul invited you over tonight. Let's skip the pleasantries. Tell us what happened yesterday."

I kept pacing, cleared my throat and recited what happened starting with the floating black fist. Raul watched me. He crouched by the fireplace and played with the poker.

"When we entered the schoolyard yesterday morning, a disembodied black fist appeared out of nowhere. It hung over our heads and blocked us from entering the school building."

Silence greeted my first statement. Raul took a deep breath, and released it. Abuelito found a spot above my head and stared at it. Abuelita twisted her hands and dropped her gaze. "Go on," she managed to say.

"It dropped paper scraps on us."

I shut my eyes tight and waited. Abuelito cleared his throat, and then coughed twice, dry rasping hacks. I didn't see what Abuelita did, but I imagined she stood up and then dropped down on to the sofa. I didn't hear Raul move. He must've stayed put out of harm's way, I thought. I plowed on.

"A piece of chalk flew into the air and wrote three sentences on the board. The eraser rose into the air. It removed the sentences from the board and fell to the blackboard's shelf underneath."

This time, no one moved. I hurried on wanting to finish my recitation before I lost my nerve altogether.

"A lit match turned the fire sprinkler on in our class. We had to leave. The fire alarm went off, and the fire department and sheriff arrived in the parking lot. I finished in a rushed squeak. "Our classroom was the only one affected. The rest of the school was okay."

This time, I kept my eyes opened. Raul beamed. He got to his feet and joined me standing in front of his grandparents.

"I told yo."

It wasn't all right. Abuelito drew himself up to his full height of 5'11. His voice thundered. Spittle struck me on the cheek.

"Garbage! Don't expect me to sit here another minute and listen to this! Rising chalk! Black fists hanging in space! Fire sprinklers turning themselves on! What next? UFO's? Bigfoot? The Loch Ness Monster? Garbage! All of it!"

Abuelito stomped out of the room leaving Raul, his wife and I speechless. Abuelita rose from the couch and took two steps out of the room. She stopped and twisted her body. "Did Eldertress appear to you, too?"

Raul sucked in his breath.

"Yes, when I blacked out."

"Thought so, sit down both of you. I'll get Miguel. He... doesn't...disbelieve you. He...just...doesn't...like it being said out loud. He's afraid of the spirits."

Did I hear Abuelita right? Abuelito afraid of the spirits? I stole a glance at Raul. He stood open mouthed. Abuelita just admitted that ghosts exist, and Abuelito was afraid of them?

Raul's grandfather stomped back into the living room followed by Abuelita.

"Do your parents know?

"Nope, it just started," I said.

"They must be told."

"Her granma knows," Raul said.

Abuelita raised her eyes. I met them.

"Granma guessed. It seems." I stopped at a loss for words. I didn't know how much I should tell them. Would Abuelito explode again? Would Abuelita believe me? I stood there half tempted to explain, but didn't.

"Don't speak to them," Abuelita said.

"What time is it?" I said.

"Almost eight-thirty," Raul said.

"Gotta go."

Raul took me by the arm and dragged me out of the house. The door opened and closed behind us. Proctectora called after me.

"Good-night."

Chapter Nine

Thursday

I awoke that morning to the beating of drums in my head. Something was perched on the top of the headboard of my bed. I felt it. My body swayed with the beat. I dressed in my school uniform—a tailored white shirt, navy blue pleated skirt and socks. I wore my pink sneakers with the bright red shoelaces.

When I got to the kitchen, Granma was standing in the middle of the room. She slammed an aluminum slotted spoon against one of Momma's cast iron frying pans. I covered my ears and tried shutting out the harsh sound.

"Whassup?"

"Thought I saw a rat," she said.

I scoured the floor, counters and cabinets with my eyes, looking for any sign of them. Small brown pellets littered the floor by the garbage can. I followed them. They stopped by the utility closet. I opened the door, peered in, and jumped. On one of the white lined papered shelves sat a fat rat, gnawing and foraging. It held a kernel in its front paws.

"Granma!"

She pushed me from the doorway. The rat fled. I leaped to the counter and hauled myself up on it. I tucked my legs underneath me, my eyes wide like saucers. I heard Granma chuckle.

"Stay put. I'll get Malcolm. He's bettah at this kind of thin' than yo' are."

Granma pattered out of the kitchen. I glared at the rat's droppings. It had disappeared into some nook. Five minutes later Malcolm bounced in. "Granma says a rat attacked you."

I nodded and pointed with a trembling finger. Malcolm crouched down and studied the floor. He got back up onto his feet and went into the broom closet. He returned, with Poppa's shovel resting over his shoulder. He bent down. His eyes examined the spaces under the cabinets. He whistled and brought the shovel down hard on the floor. The tile that Granma had glued two days ago unstuck and flipped up. The rat dashed across the floor. Malcolm scrambled to his feet and pounced after it. It dashed into the closet. Malcolm followed.

"Gottcha!" I heard Malcolm shout. He came out. The limp rat dangled from his fingers. I rolled my eyes and gagged.

"Get rid of it."

Malcolm swung the rat by its tail. He ducked out of the room. I heard the back screen door slam shut. Minutes later Malcolm returned. I didn't see the shovel.

"Bettah wash yo' hands. Rats are diseased."

He laughed and waltzed to the sink. Turning on the faucet, we watched the water spew out. Granma pushed her way back into the kitchen. "Thought I saw yo' outside. Killed the rat?"

Malcolm nodded "yes."

I untangled my feet and slid down from the counter. "Thanks Malcolm." I shivered. "I hate rats!"

"Breakfast?"

Granma still held the frying pan and slotted spoon in her hand. She put them on the range top and took out the plastic pancake bottle. Malcolm handed her the bottle of oil from the refrigerator. She poured the oil into the pan, coating it lightly. Turning on the electric stove, I collected the silverware from the drawer and set the table. Malcolm got out plates and glasses.

We sat down at the table. The kitchen grew warm. Granma flipped the pancakes. Malcolm and I watched her as she seemed to put on a show for us. Five minutes later Granma piled the pancakes on our plates. We ate in silence. The clock rang out the hour.

"Dag naggit! We're gonna be late again," I groaned.

The doorbell chimed.

"I'll get it," Malcolm said.

He hurried out of the kitchen, his milk cup half full.

"He'll finish his milk at dinner. Mama doesn' make 'em drink it. He'll just spit it up."

Granma cleared our plates from the table, wordless. Raul sauntered into the kitchen, with Malcolm at his heels. "Ready? Morning, Mrs. Kingsley."

"Raul," Granma said, acknowledging him this time. "Wha' time yo' and yar brothahh get home, Anna Mae?"

"Two-thirty for Malcolm. I'll be home by three-thirty."

"Be sure tha' yo' do."

"I'll make sure that she does."

I squirmed. "Gotta go."

I ran into the hallway, picked up my backpack and headed towards the door. Malcolm trailed me. Raul brought up the rear. Granma plodded out of the kitchen.

We waved good-bye and left. Granma made it to the door and shut it.

"Race you to the tracks!" Malcolm challenged.

We jumped off the porch stoop and galloped down the road. My backpack thumped on my back. We got to the tracks in six minutes flat. My stomach flipped. I slowed down to a trot. Malcolm clutched his stomach. "Can we...walk...the...rest of the way? I don't feel so hot."

Raul locked eyes with me. "Feeling sick too?"

"A bit queasy. Can we walk?"

A commuter train wooshed by and blasted us with three sharp, ear-splitting whistle bursts. We scurried across the tracks once it had passed us. I checked my watch. "We're gonna be late again. That's the eight-ten train bound for Atlanta!"

Chapter Ten

Worried, Raul checked his own watch. There was no sense in him being late with us.

"Yo'd bettah go 'head. Malcolm and me, we'll be fine. One of us should be on time."

Raul turned and raced off. Malcolm and I followed at a slower pace. Halfway to school, Malcolm bent over. His tongue lolled out between his lips. He burped twice. Like a humpback woman, Malcolm hurried to the side of the road. He heaved twice. Pancake chunks, syrup, and milk spattered the grass.

In sympathy, my own stomach flipped. I closed my eyes. The sound of retching continued. Fingers clutched my arm. "I'm finished, Anna Mae," Malcolm finally said.

Shrugging off my backpack, I opened the flap and took out a pack of tissues. I took one out and handed it to Malcolm. He wiped his lips and hands with it. "Give it to me. Don' want to litter." I folded the soiled tissue in a clean one, and then stuffed both in my skirt pocket.

"Bettah?"

"Yeah, much bettah."

I checked my watch. "Let's go. It's almost eight-twenty."We trotted the rest of the way. I glanced at Malcolm, expecting him to up-chuck again, but he didn't. Malcolm and I made it to school by eight thirty-five.

"Bettah get ovah to the nurse's station and get a pass. Yo' still look piqued."

"I'll be okay. Principal Teddy might want me to change into something less smelly though."

"His call, not ours. See yo' latah."

Malcolm hung a left off the hallway and ran down the steps. The nurse's station was in the basement next to the gymnasium. I bumped into a senior hall monitor. She took a whiff and waved me away. I trotted down the hall and came to homeroom. Principal Teddy walked out of the door, lifted his eyebrows, but didn't say a word. He pointed towards the classroom. I opened the door, slunk in and crawled into my seat. The class tittered.

"You're late!" Ms. Yolanda said.

"Malcom got sick on the way to school this morning."Her nose wrinkled. "You smell. Got sick, too, this morning?"

"My brother threw up on the way to school." I kept my eyes on the floor.

Ms. Yolanda shrugged. "Go to your seat. I'll mark you tardy. One more time though and I'll be forced to send a note home to your parents."

"Yes, Ma'am," I said and retreated to my desk-chair and sat down. I got back up and this time I removed my backpack, stowing it underneath my chair.

"Wondered when you'd show." Raul whispered behind his left hand.

Ms. Yolanda started roll call. "Josephina Derby."

"Here."

"Robert Ashley III."

"Here."

"Martha Jennings."

"Here."

"Anna Mae Botts."

"Present."

"Raul Garcia."

"Here."

"Stanley Paxton."

He didn't answer.

Ms. Yolanda repeated his name. "Stanley Paxton?" Again, he didn't answer. She looked up and stared at Stanley's empty desk. Her eyes shifted to Lola Simms' desk. Lola was missing, as were the rest of Stanley's gang. I saw Ms. Yolanda's eyes scan the room. I noticed that Catherine Harper was also missing.

"Wait right here," she said, but the room suddenly filled with black smoke. Coughing, Ms. Yolanda covered her mouth and nostrils with her right hand. Someone screamed. It was me. I pointed towards the ceiling, where flames licked it.

Through the flames I saw the ceiling start to buckle. Wendy started blubbering. I exploded. "Shut up! Raul do something! We've got to get outta here!"

Raul stood up and climbed up on his desk. "Anna Mae, you lead the class outta here. I'll take care of Ms. Yolanda. Don't run. Get into a single line. Leave your stuff behind."

Collecting myself, I forced my feet to move towards the classroom door. "Follow me!"

Raul jumped off his desk and ran towards Ms. Yolanda. He grabbed her by the forearm and dragged her towards me. "Get going. No time to waste."

I pushed opened the door. Heat from the hallway forced me back. The kids pushed forward. I fell into the hallway. The kids streamed behind me, running towards the exit doors.

Behind me I heard Martha wail. "I can't see!"

I turned and ran back in to the classroom. Martha stood frozen in the middle of the room. Her arms flailed in front of her. The smoke gathered in pockets. Covering my nose, I ran back into the room and grabbed Martha by her arm. "Come on. We don't got all day." I dragged her from the room and shoved her through the doorway. The flames inched closer. The heat licked my face. The flames grew larger as a fresh breeze sprang up from nowhere.

The boys were gone. Martha wasn't the only one left scared and disoriented in that room. The Asian and black kids milled. I barged back into the room, angrier than hell. I had to get their attention. I threw a tantrum, stamping my feet and banging my hands against the wall. "Listen! Get down on your hands and knees. Start crawling. Keep your head down and your nose close to the floor. The smoke rises. You can breathe better. When you get to the door, get to your feet, stand up, form a line and walk to the nearest fire exit. Don't run. You'll scare the younger kids."

Someone slapped me on the back. Raul came up from behind me. He batted my ankle. Ms. Yolanda and Raul were on their knees. They crawled forward. When the rest of the kids saw Ms. Yolanda crawling towards the door, they dropped to their knees and followed.

I started coughing. Tears ran down my face. The room was so full of smoke. Through the haze, I dropped to my knees and felt for anyone's ankle or shoe. I felt fresh air brush against my face. Blind, I aimed for the doorway. Drums started beating in my ears. A rhythmic message, it was telling me something. I followed the beats out of the smoke-filled room and out into the hallway.

"You made it!" I heard the Protectora' thin voice inside my head.

Ms. Yolanda stood in the hallway. Beside her, Raul stood, his face all smudged with soot. The rest of the kids waited in the hallway in a single line. Ms. Yolanda glanced at me. "Anyone else?"

I shook my head "no." Ms. Yolanda led the class down the blackened hallway. Something forced me to look back. All I could see at first was smoke, flames, but then—a floating black chain and an overlarge black fist.

The fire horn blared. Other students joined us in the hallway. We hurried out into the parking lot. I heard, as did everyone else, Principal Teddy's voice screaming over the school loudspeaker. "This is not a drill. Everyone leave the building. I repeat, this is not a fire drill!"

Then silence. Principal Teddy stopped speaking. The speaker went dead. In the parking lot, along with the rest of the students and teachers, I watched the building burn. Ms. Yolanda counted heads, as did the rest of the teachers. I noticed that each one counted more than once.

"Look!" Raul shouted.

We all turned and faced him, even the teachers. He pointed towards the school. A thousand eyes followed his finger. The entire school was engulfed in flames. Windows exploded. Glass flew and shards scattered all over the ground. Smoke poured out of the roof, while flames licked the sky.

I saw the elementary school students stumble out of their doors. Each student fell on the grass, hugging their stomachs. Black smoke billowed through the open doors. The flames flickered through shattered windows and shot upwards. I rubbed my eyes. I thought I saw three students standing on the roof. Naw! Who would be that stupid? A boy dragged me back into the parking lot. I pushed his hand off.

"Yo' getting' too close to the buildin'. Malcolm's okay, if tha's who yo' were lookin' for."

I turned. Raul. rubbed his hands.

"How do yo' know?"

"I just know."

"Don' believe yo'," I said.

I searched the school grounds and didn't see him. Ms.Yolanda waved Raul and me back towards the class. I ignored her and kept looking for Malcolm. Principal Teddy appeared from out of nowhere. He looked a mess. His suit jacket was torn and singed. His shirt collar was open at the top. Blood bruises darkened his eyes and cheeks. His hands were blistered from the heat and flames.

"Is everyone out?" Ms. Yolanda called to him.

"I think so. The teachers are counting students."

Thirty feet up, the window from the bell tower blew out. It fell and smashed on the ground. Principal Teddy shielded his eyes and peered up. Four students stood on the thin, narrow ledge under the empty window slot. Orange and red flames shot out. They danced as they dodged the flickering fire tongues.

In the distance, fire trucks wailed. An ambulance arrived, along with three fire trucks. They roared into the parking lot with a police escort. I turned and watched as eight firefighters, some of them women, jumped from each fire truck, already suited up. They rushed towards the window, carrying a net in their hands.

Principal Teddy left the parking lot and scurried toward the building. He lifted his head and called through cupped hands. "Stanley Paxton?"

Transfixed, I stared, mouth open, lips parted. My head reeled. How did Principal Teddy know it was Stanley Paxton up there on the bell tower's roof? I shook my head and glanced at Raul. He shrugged. Ms. Yolanda hurried towards the building.

Things happened quickly after that. The fire chief roared through a bullhorn, "Jump!"

Like a sportscaster's reciting a play-by-play, I heard Raul call out the entire event to a waiting school. "A kid just jumped from the ledge. I think it was Stanley Paxton. Yup, he fell into the middle of the net and bounced. Two firemen helped him out. A sheriff has taken Stanley into custody.

"An Emergency Medical Technician has joined them. They're taking him to the ambulance. Must be treating him for burns. Uh oh, they put an oxygen mask over his face. A technician is taking his blood pressure.

"Here comes Ms. Yolanda. She's running towards the ambulance. Nothing more there. Will you look at that? The fire chief and Principal Teddy are waving at the other kids to jump too.

"There goes the next kid. Hmm, looks a lot like Lola. She landed in the middle of the net too. Principal Teddy took her hand and helped her out of the net. He's talking to her. Wonder what he's saying? There she goes. A police woman is leading her to the ambulance too."

"Wow! Wouldja look at that? They're jumping off the ledge one by one, like parachuters. Awesome! Hey, Catherine Harper! Way to go! Two fire folks have helped her outta the net. There goes Joey. The fire chief led all three of them to the ambulance. I guess it's the EMT's turn now, checkin' 'em for cuts, burns, and shock. Hey, Anna Mae, yar missin' all the action."

"What 'bout Malcolm?" I wanted to scream. I looked for Malcolm, but I still couldn't see him. I couldn't see his teacher, Mr. Santos either. *Where was he?* I shivered and crept away from Raul and the rest of the class. I needed to find my little brother. He was more important to me than life itself.

Without thinking, I yelled out to him, "Malcolm! Answer me, damn it!"

I ran towards the other side of the parking lot, screaming his name. The coach tried blocking me, but his arms slipped. The girls' gym teacher tackled me, but I stepped out of her embrace. I wove and dodged my way around the teachers and two custodians. I had to find my little brother—no ifs, ands or buts about it.

I kept running. My breath came in short spurts. My legs churned the ground. I couldn't stop myself. "Malcolm! Where the hell are you?"

It was Mr. Santos who finally caught me. I struggled in his arms. He smothered me in his embrace until I stopped fighting him. He looked me straight in the face. "You're brother is okay, Anna Mae. He's sitting on the curb with the rest of my class. We wanted to keep the elementary kids separate from the middle school. Calm down. You know how scared some of these kids are. See? He's sitting right over there. Why don't you go over and hug him, and then walk back to your class. Fair enough?"

I sighed, and then hurried to the curb where Malcolm sat with his friends.

"You okay?"

"Right as rain," he said.

"I just wanted to make sure. I was scared for you."

Malcolm hugged me. I felt better and trudged back to Raul.

Black smoke continued to rise from the building. Flames leaped higher and higher. I could feel the heat. Ms. Yolanda and the other teachers kept moving us further and further away from the burning building. The police and fire people set up some yellow crime scene tape around the building. Everyone kept asking the same question: "How did it start?"

I knew by the way the building burned that school would be closed tomorrow. Raul threw his arm around my shoulders and hugged me. I squirmed out of his embrace and stepped away from him. I bumped into Lola Simms. Her hair hung down, matted. I smelled burned flesh and hair. My nose wrinkled. I watched her as she sagged to the ground.

"You okay? Raul, go get Ms. Yolanda. Lola fell."

Raul dashed off towards Ms. Yolanda. I sat by the fallen girl. Her face was burned in several places. She moaned and swayed. I didn't know what to do or how to touch her. Her blouse was ripped and stained. Her skirt hung in tatters. I reached out and tried embracing her, but she pulled away from me.

Ms. Yolanda ran over to us, with Raul at her heels. She kneeled by Lola and took her right hand. "What's wrong?"

I got the feeling that Ms. Yolanda was asking me rather than Lola. "I'm not sure. She just fell over."

Ms. Yolanda stared into Lola's face. She nodded and started crying. With loud sniffs and short coughing bouts, Lola was convincing. "You're not...you're not taking me back to the sheriff, are you?" Her voice trembled. She kept crying, sniffling, and coughed every now and then. I watched her performance, fascinated. Ms. Yolanda answered her softly.

"No, but Principal Teddy wants to speak with you." Ms. Yolanda took off her white cotton crocheted sweater and hung it around Lola's shoulders. Together, they stood up. Ms. Yolanda walked off with Lola. She hunched over. Ms. Yolanda's sweater sleeves swung empty at her side. They strolled towards Principal Teddy. He limped alongside the fire marshal and the sheriff.

They all met in the middle of the parking lot. Principal Teddy escorted Lola to one of the waiting squad cars. They ducked their heads and climbed into the car. I would've given anything to hear what Principal Teddy said to Lola, but I was too far away to hear anything. Raul held onto my hand and made sure I didn't follow after them.

"I'd give anything to hear Lola's side of the story. What do yo' think?"

Raul squeezed my hand. "It has nothin' to do with us."

"Wha' 'bout the fire? Aren' yo' curious as to how it was started?"

Raul shrugged. "That's easy. It was the black fist."

I looked at him as if he was crazy. "No way it could've done that."

"Oh no? What about yesterday and the fire sprinkler? It just happened to go off by itself? Get a life, Anna Mae! The fist set it off yesterday too. Just a trial run. Today was the real thing."

I stared at the school and wondered how much longer it would take to put out the fire. Sirens wailed. Two more fire trucks roared into the lot, with more fire personnel than I'd ever seen in my life. Water poured from fire hoses and onto the building. The flames refused to die. Martha and Wendy joined us.

"Who do ya think started that fire?" Martha asked.

I shrugged. "Yar asking me? How would I know?"

"Guess!" Martha moved off, but she kept staring at me and shaking her head. I didn't say a thing. There wasn't anyone else standing close to us, but I didn't like the way Martha joined each group of kids and whispered lies into their ears.

Wendy walked over to Martha and whispered into her ear. Martha said at the top of her voice, "I don't believe it for a minute." She stared at me and then pointed. All of the kids turned and faced me. Their faces screwed up and their eyes narrowed. They watched as Martha straightened her shoulders, and then in a deadpan voice shot out her arm and pointed at me. "She started the fire!"

Tongue-tied, I spluttered. Martha scared me. She smelled of fear. Raul approached me and stood by my side. He groped for my hand.

"Word's out, we're to go home. The school's totaled."

I sighed and found his hand. I clasped it. "I didn't hear anyone say that."

"How could you?" Raul retorted. "You were busy fighting with Martha."

"We're not fightin'."

"Yo' sure? It seems like she's accusin' yo' of startin' the fire. Didja?" His eyes narrowed. "It seemed like something to me. I saw your face. It crumbled"

"I don' know wha' yar talkin' 'bout."

"Fine with me, but 'fore yo' go hysterical on me, let's face facts. Pit Bull, Lola, Catherine, and a bunch of kids jumped out of the bell tower window. The sheriff and Principal Teddy took them to the ambulance. The EMT's checked them out. Lola joined us and falls to the ground. Ms. Yolanda took her to the principal. Principal Teddy escorted Lola to the police cruiser. Martha and Wendy joined us. Martha accused you of starting the fire. Did I leave anything out?"

"Malcolm, I rushed over to find him."

"So you did. You found him and was sent back by his teacher, Mr. Santos. Did I miss anything else?"

I stood there, frozen, not able to think. I kept seeing Martha's and Wendy's distorted faces. The rest of the class didn't look too friendly either. Raul dropped my hand. "I don't want you to accuse me of acting unfairly."

Behind me, someone bumped me. I turned. It was Malcolm. "Come on, Anna Mae. Mr. Santos says we can go home. School's closed for today."

I looked around the parking lot. All of the kids stepped away from us as if we were diseased. Even Raul seemed uncertain. Malcolm looked up. "Here comes your teacher. Let's see if she says the same thing," Malcolm said.

Ms. Yolanda walked straight towards the middle of the parking lot. She cupped her hands and spoke between them. "School is closed until further notice. You may all go home."

"See?" Malcolm said. He patted my arm. "Let's go 'fore they change their minds." He pulled at my arm. I watched Ms. Yolanda. Her arms fell to her side. She seemed to wilt before my eyes. Without thinking what I was doing, I marched up to her and hugged her tight. She sniffed and coughed. "Thanks, I needed that." She smiled and then stooped down. "I'm glad you hugged me. It makes what I have to say easier somehow."

I stiffened. She lowered her head. "Anna Mae, a serious charge was leveled at you. You've been accused of setting that fire. The student who told us said that he saw you deliberately loiter in the schoolyard, waiting for the late bell to ring. He said you rolled in the dirt and then took garbage out of the can and rubbed it all over your body. What do you have to say?"

I saw the rest of the kids step back and away from us. Martha stepped forward and separated herself from the class. Like an ancient prophetess, she uttered her fateful words. "Ask her why she was so late coming to class. Ask her what her brother was doing by the gym early this morning. I would love to hear her excuse."

I shivered. Raul stirred. Marko, a friend of Pit Bull's, raised his hand and spoke. "Her brother, Malcolm, he came late too. How come?"

I pulled Malcolm closer to me. He bristled. "I upchucked on the way to school. I went to the nurse. She gave me a pass."

Raul stepped further away. For a minute I thought he would raise both his hands and make the sign of the cross. Tears clouded my eyes. Malcolm growled. I pulled him back. "It doesn't mattah. He really isn' one of us."

Mr. Santos stepped out of the crowd of kids. He walked up to us and patted Malcolm on his shoulder. "I'll drive you two home. Malcolm, you know my car. Take Anna Mae there." He turned and walked up to Raul. "A minute of your time, son."

Malcolm pushed me towards Mr. Santos' parked car. I saw that the rest of the school kids watched as Mr. Santos ambled up to Raul. Mr. Santos towered over Raul. He stooped and said something. I strained to hear his words, but I couldn't. Malcolm opened the car door and shoved me inside. He got in beside me and slammed the door shut.

Mr. Santos walked to the car alone. He pulled the door open and slid in. He turned the key in the ignition. The car spurted to life. I turned and looked out the window. Raul stood, hunched by himself, in the middle of the parking lot. Martha stood by his side, waving.

Chapter Eleven

Mr. Santos dropped us off at the door. It stood open. Granma stood with her arms crossed in front of her chest as if she already knew what happened at school. That couldn't be, yet I had the feeling that she was waiting there on purpose. She sent Malcolm and me to our rooms. With her back turned, she didn't see us. Malcolm and me, we stood in the hallway straining our ears.

I heard Mr. Santos' voice murmuring behind us. He didn't say anything that I didn't already know. We retreated down the hallway and into the kitchen—our sanctuary. I dumped my backpack on the floor. Malcolm headed toward the refrigerator and took out the plastic gallon of milk. I went to the food pantry and removed a tin of raisin-oatmeal cookies.

Our vigil seemed eternal, but I heard the front door close. Granma plodded into the kitchen. Malcolm stopped gulping his milk and put the glass on the table. I stopped chewing my cookie and waited. I licked a cookie wedge from my lips. Granma pulled out one of the dinette chairs and sat down, her fingers twisted and intertwined.

"It finally happened."

"What...finally...happened?" Malcolm squeaked.

"I'm talkin' t' yar sistah. The fire...yar school is done burned down. Raul turned his back on yo'."

I swallowed.

"Why don'ja take your milk and cookies and watch TV?"

Malcolm glanced at Granma. "Okie Dokie."

Malcolm poured more milk into his glass and took the cookie tin with him. Granma never said a word. He left in a huff. Granma's eyes rested on me. "When I was a young'un, not much oldah than yo', I saw thin's. My momma hushed me and told me nevah t' tell Poppa 'bout wha' I saw. I was not t' tell anyone. I told my momma's mothahh. She knew I spoke true. She told me t' keep a special book and write down wha' I saw. My Grannie was a healah.

"She told me t' place X's next t' the thin's tha' I saw what came true, and O's for the thin's tha't didn' come true. I did as I was told."

I stopped breathing and then released my breath. It sounded like a hiss. Granma kept talking as if she was in a trance.

"My Grannie told me there were four kinds of sights: seein' thin's 'fore they happen'; seein' thin's from a great distant like people, places, and stuff; seein' thin's tha' are far off; and seein' thin's tha' were dead like haints, angels, fairies, and othah people's souls." She dug into her apron pockets and brought up a battered and tattered book. It had no cover, except for a piece of tape with her name printed in block letters on top. She laid it on the table and pushed it towards me.

"This is for yo'. My grannie gave it t' me when I was a littah oldah than yo'. Keep it by yo'. It's t' protect yo'."

I gulped. Granma looked up. Her eyes pierced mine. "It seems tha' yo' have the sight. Yo' momma don'. Yo' poppa ain't too happah 'bout it, but he leaves me be. He's 'fraid yo' take aftah me. He's right. Yo' do."

"But...but...you don't believe in haints!"

"It 'pends how yo' wan' t' look at it. I just wantah t' see if yo' took aftah me or not. Can' make no 'stakes 'bout it."

"And Malcolm?"

Granma shook her head. "Boy's don' get the sight...less they seek it."

"It skipped yar momma. Yar aunt got it, but, she went 'way. Yo' momma and poppa dote on yo' bros, but I waitah. I knew yo' were smartah. 'Sides, yo' played mostly with boys. Tha' scared 'em."

"I like boys."

"Tha's wha' bothahh 'em. Yo' best friend is Raul, not Catherine, Martha, or Wendy—wha's their last name? I waited for yo' t' ask. Yo' had question marks written all ovah yar face, but yo' kept it t' yoself."

"Yo' knew 'bout the fire."

"I knew 'bout it since I first got here. I knew 'bout Pit Bull. Don' glare at me, chile! I tired tellin' yo'. Yo' weren' payin' no mind t' me. My grannie showed me how t' handle it just like I'm doin' now. One way is t' sit still and think quiet thoughts. She also told me how t' 'tect myself from the spirit world."

My thoughts tumbled. I stared at the book. Hesitant, I reached out. With fingertips, I drew the book towards me. I looked at it. It held so many answers for me, I just didn't know where to start. Granma smiled. Right then I hated her. "Raul left me and Malcolm standin' by ourselves. He thinks Malcolm and me, we're involved."

"Raul is yo' best friend. He likes yo', but he's scared of yo', too. Don' think 'bout it."

"I hate 'em too!"

"Hate is..." Granma stopped herself, and then

continued as if I hadn't spoken at all. "Raul is a boy-man. He ain't lookin' at yo' like a friend, but as a grown woman."

"Yo' mad!" I laughed.

Granma's smile tightened.

"Come on, Granma. Get real. Raul? He's a chile."

"Old 'nough t' love. Men 'tect their women. Don' laugh at 'em. He's doin' the best he knows how."

I shook my head. "Not anymore. Yo' should've seen 'em. We're dirt t' 'em."

Granma smiled her Cheshire cat smile. "Just yo' wait. He'll come back. They always do. Can' keep 'way, even if they tried." This time she laughed outright.

"Don' lose any sleep ovah it. I came this wintah cuz I was needed. Yo' wait. The wind will turn soon. Yo' got bettah thin's t' worry 'bout."

Her words chilled me. I picked up the paper napkin and blew my nose. Granma's catlike eyes refocused. She covered the back of my hand with her own. "Listen t' me. Go int' the shed and close the door. Lay down on yar bed and close out the world. Take the book with yo'. Yar goin' t' need it."

"How do you do shut out the world?"

"Close yar eyes. Shut yar ears. Pick a spot yo' love t' sit durin' the summah. Focus on that."

"Now?"

"No bettah time. Malcolm's watchin' cartoons. He ain't goin' nowhere."

I grabbed the book and got up from the chair. I hurried through my bedroom and into the shed. I kicked the door shut. The latch caught and held the door tight. I ran and jumped on the bed. It sagged. I lay down with my arms by my sides. Closing my eyes, I shut out the drone of the television and the kitchen sounds. The chirping birds faded. The room became still. I heard the dripping faucet. I tuned that out. I waited.

Chapter Twelve

"Fleeing south, I heed the call, weighed down by doubt and fear. I run. I hide. Blue uniforms appear out of nowhere. I alone give away millions meant for other hands. I have lost. Betrayed, I run for my life. My home... My family... My people...Lost forever along the path of liberty, too freely purchased."

As I relax, I retreated into myself and felt nothing except the constant thumping of my heart.

"Buried deep, golden coins, scattered in haste. Deceptive, bright by the light, they trick the eyes, hiding the flight of the French gold once borrowed, and now lost."

A coarse voice seemed to speak through me. "Broken free and in flight, I soared above my body and looked down at a brown speck on the bed. The blue sky and passing clouds greeted me as I flew. Gliding, I rode the wind. Moist coolness brushed my feather tips as I dove for a forgotten crumb. Wheeling high in the air, I flew with my bit of food tight in my beak. I landed on the shoulder of the one I protected, hiding my true identity."

"Follow the path that Davis and his Confederate Cabinet traveled, his flight from Richmond one week before General Lee's surrender at Appomattox. Davis entrusted the French and treasury gold to a Captain Lot Abraham en route. It proved too much for the captain. He and his men stole the gold and fled through Wilkes County.

"A man, dressed as a woman, broke into a clearing. Federal troops in blue uniforms and carrying rifles arrested him, mocking and laughing at him.

"Eight wagons pulled by mule teams lumbered into view. Two Negro soldiers sat in each of the wagons. Bags were stowed inside the wagons. All the soldiers were armed with rifles.

"Union soldiers searched for fleeing Confederate families. One husband forced his wife and children to take an alternate route. Fifty miles later, he visited a solitary plantation, riding a horse. The man bolted when he was attacked. He left on foot. His horse forgotten in flight, was caught by a dozen Union soldiers." I read carefully, feeling as if I were actually there.

An eighteen-year-old brunette woman spoke to her father as she pawed through the trunk of golden coins.

"See, Father?" she said. "I told you he would give it to you. He trusts you. Where shall we hide it?"

Her father slammed the trunk's lid down and locked it with his key.

Her father disappeared for two hours. When he returned, three darkies followed behind with shovels and pickaxes.

"Be quiet and tell no one. You haven't seen me today, Mary Anne. Understand? You haven't seen me since I deserted. That's all you need know."

Three darkies carried the trunk between them. I heard them leave. Mary Anne shivered and clutched her shawl around her shoulders. Minutes later, she heard the rush of feet and hooves in the front yard. She stared out the window.

Thirty soldiers streamed into the front yard. Mary Anne saw the blue uniform of a Yankee major. She watched him dismount and throw his reins to a small darkie. He hurried up the stairs.

Mary Anne heard someone knock on the door. She hesitated and wondered where her father was. The knocking increased. Mary Anne walked to the door. She opened it just as the major was about to strike it with the hilt of his sword.

"May I help you?" she drawled, watching the major's face. It was impassive.

"Is your father home, Miss?"

"He ran off," Mary Anne said, her lips pressed together.

"You here all alone?"

"Not alone. Some darkies still remain."

The major bent his head closer to Mary Anne's. "Seen any gold, Miss?"

Mary Anne narrowed her eyes. She glared at the major. "I haven't seen any gold here, Sir. As you can see, my home's been stripped of everything, just a shell of its former splendor. If you like, please inspect it yourself."

The major paused. He lifted one boot, but he hesitated.

"Sir!" one of his men shouted. "We've found something in the barn!"

The major bowed. "Until next time."

He walked out of her house and out of her line of sight. Mary Anne walked back into the grand room. She sank into a chair, her dress spreading in a circle around her. Her head ached. She wished for the comfort of her mother's hands, but there was none there—unless you counted the darkies, and they didn't exist to her.

Inside the barn, the major stared at the floor. He kneeled on it and ran his white-gloved hand through the hay strewn over the wooden planks. He searched, hoping to find what his corporal had spotted—a golden coin struck with Jefferson Davis' image on one side.

He felt something round and grabbed it. The major picked up a coin and looked at it. Was it part of the gold confiscated by Jefferson Davis?

"Keep searching. It's around here somewhere, and we'll be the richer for it."

Mary Anne noticed that the Union major and his troops didn't leave that day. They stayed all night, their torches lit. Finally, late in the morning, they left. The major bowed and saluted her. He mounted his horse while his darkie fell back and rejoined the soldiers, trotting behind their major.

She snorted. The North didn't really treat their darkies any better than the South did. Mary Anne embroidered for the remainder of the day. When the sun mellowed into dusk, she lit the lanterns. Her kitchen darkie served a poor meal of rice and beans. Mary Anne ate it hungrily. She watched as the darkie cleared the table and brought in a cup of chicory coffee.

At nine-thirty by the mantle clock, her father came home.

"Are the soldiers gone?"

"Yes, Father. They left this morning."

"Did they find anything?" he asked, with a tired smile.

Mary Anne stared at her father.

"You planted that gold coin in the barn?"

"I planted some gold coins in the barn and between here and Sandersville."

Her father laughed. It wasn't pleasant; it was more like a conspiratorial one. "They won't find much," she said.

"Enough to satisfy their greed, but no, they won't find much." He kept smiling.

Mary Anne watched her father. His secretive smile comforted her, knowing that the South had won over the Union in one thing that the Union dearly wanted: Confederate gold.

"It's late, Mary Anne. You should be in bed. I'll stand guard until daybreak. You can relieve me then. Jefferson Davis' gold is in good hands."

A foot slammed against my door. Half of me wanted to scream, "Go away!" but the other part of me, my physical self, awoke with a jerk. I rubbed my eyes and forced myself to wake up.

I slid to the floor. I staggered to the bathroom sink and turned on the faucet. I splashed cold water on my face. With wet and dripping hands, I searched for the hanging towel. I found it and pulled it off the rack.

"Anna Mae, are you awake?" Malcolm asked through the door.

I dried my face and looked in the mirror. My eyes stared back at me, and something else. I hurried out of the bathroom and opened the door.

"Granma wants you."

I tried to clear my head. Images of Mary Anne and her thoughts and actions still clogged my brain. I followed Malcolm into the kitchen. Granma sat near the table.

"Sit down, chile. There's a sheriff here wantin' t' speak with yo' 'bout the fire. I told him I wouldn' let 'em speak t' yo' without me bein' here with yo'."

Malcolm gripped the back of Granma's chair. "I'll stay with her, Granma."

Granma winked at him. "Thank yo' chile, but I believe tha' yo' sistah wants me t' stay with her. Ain't tha' so, chile? Yo' do know why he's here?"

"I know."

"Malcolm, go back int' the livin' room and go watch yo' cartoons a bit more. I'll call yo' should we need t'. Yo' wait here while I go and git our guest."

Granma left the kitchen. I sat down at the table, wishing I'd brought that book back with me. She returned with the sheriff. He stood six-foot three inches tall and wore his blues like my poppa did. I looked up and gulped. His eyes were set together. His eyebrows grew together. His hands were larger than Poppas. I wished he would just get it over with. I couldn't see his eyes. He wore mirrored sunglasses. The sheriff twirled the chair next to me and set it backwards. He sat down, his legs straddled in either direction.

"Anna Mae Botts?"

"Yes, sir." I waited. I hadn't expected another black man on the force. Poppa never spoke about his work. He preferred to keep his personal life separate from his police work. I wondered if he was married and had children, and why he decided to work in Lowry instead of Atlanta, the city friendly to black people.

"There was a fire at your school today. We suspect arson. The fire marshals inspected the site. They smelled gasoline fumes and found bits and pieces of charred newspaper. I've interviewed four students. Their versions pretty much sound the same. I heard you and your brother were late coming into class this morning. I need to hear your side of the story."

The sheriff removed a miniature tape recorder from his shirt pocket. "I need to record your testimony."

Granma stared at the recorder. She pointed at it. "Must yo'?"

The sheriff never looked up. "It's customary to record testimony when interviewing a possible suspect. My job is to find the truth. Anna Mae is a suspect."

"My gran'chile don' lie." She folded her arms across her chest. Her face remained impassive.

"I'm not here to dispute whether she lies or not. I want the truth. It's protocol. Begin," the sheriff said.

I saw my image in his sunglasses. I felt small and mean.

"Can you take off your sunglasses, sir?"

The man removed his glasses. He wore a glass eye.

Chapter Thirteen

"Is that better?"

Granma pulled the stool from the utility shed. She plopped down and watched, mesmerized. I stared at his glass eye—blue against white. I studied my fingers and a real bad feeling washed over me.

The sheriff pushed the button on the recorder. I watched as the wheels turned inside it. "Ready?"

I gulped. I didn't know where to start. I opened my mouth and forced each word out. The sheriff leaned forward. He placed his left hand on my right knee. Granma's head jerked. I steeled myself and hid my hands under my legs. The sheriff nodded, cleared his throat and started. He held the recorder up to his lips. They brushed against the hidden microphone.

"Anna Mae Botts, you've been accused of setting the school on fire this morning. It's been alleged that your nine-year-old brother, Malcolm Botts, helped you set the fire. Your accusers are Christina Harper, John Fry, Mark Somers, Stuart Langston, Herman Potts, and Joey Fritz. The fire marshal spoke to Lola Simms and Stanley Paxton. They accused you of setting that fire. These students are willing to testify that you deliberately and maliciously set the fire. They're prepared to swear in court that you boasted about setting the fire without getting caught because your father was a police sergeant."

My head whirled. They all lied to save their sweet butts because I saw Pit Bull cower in front of a disembodied floating black fist. My eyes teared up. "It's not true. I didn't do it"

"Your classmates are prepared to state that you arrived in homeroom after the late bell rang."

"Not 'cause I set a fire."

"Why were you late?"

"Malcolm threw up on the way to school."

"You expect me to believe that? Arson is a serious charge."

"I didn't do it!"

Granma butted in. I guess she couldn't take it. "If my young'un says she didn' do it, she didn' do it."

"Ma'am, I've heard plenty of kids swear in court that they didn't do something only to be proved guilty. I'm just trying to get to the bottom of this and lick it in the bud. I don't know your granddaughter. I'm going on what her classmates tell me. They're the ones who know her better than anybody...except maybe her parents, you, and her brother."

"Would a best friend do?"

The sheriff shook his head. "Under normal circumstances, maybe, but arson isn't normal. It's a federal offense—a felony. I've got to get to the bottom of this." The sheriff stared at me. "Why don't you start at the beginning instead of at the middle. There must be a reason why these kids are lying...if...they...are...lying."

"When my best friend, my baby brother and I got to the school yard on the first day of school, a large black floating fist blocked our path."

The sheriff permitted himself a smile. "You believe you saw a ghost? Is that right?"

"It was real, okay? Stanley Paxton saw it too. He wet his pants."

The sheriff stared over my head. The room grew even quieter. "Go on."

"Malcolm ran off to the bathroom. Raul dragged me into school."

The sheriff cleared his throat. He lowered his eyes and held mine. "What happened to the black fist?"

"It went away." I took another gulp of air. "On the second day, a piece of chalk rose from the blackboard shelf and wrote three sentences on the board. The eraser slid off the shelf and flew up into the air. It erased the sentences. The fire sprinkler went off. It soaked me. The fire alarm rang. Everybody from the middle school left the building. The fire trucks and police came. They couldn't find anything, so they left. Ms. Yolanda led our class into the gymnasium and we had to have homeroom there. In the afternoon, Ms. Yolanda held class in the auditorium."

The sheriff slouched into the chair. He removed his hand and turned off the recorder. "Can I trouble you for a glass of water?"

"I'll get it." I jumped out of the chair and went to the cabinet. I took out two glasses—one for him and one for me. I walked to the sink and turned on the faucet. I let the water run. I tested the water with my forefinger. It got cold. I held first his glass and then mine under the faucet and filled them.

Granma got up from the stool and took both glasses from me. "Sit!" she ordered.

I sat back down in my chair. She handed the glass to the sheriff, reaching over my head. It dripped. Granma placed my glass on the table. I watched the sheriff pick up his glass and bring it to his lips. He finished the water in four gulps. I sipped my water and waited. I knew he wasn't finished with me, not by a long shot.

"Okay, the fire marshal and the police visited your school and found no one had tinkered with the fire alarm or sprinkler."

"No, no one."

"You went back to class and nothing further was done."

I shook my head. "Nothing further was done."

"What happened today?"

"Malcolm and I had pancakes for breakfast. Raul, that's my best friend, he came and picked us up. We raced to the railroad tracks. Malcolm felt sick. We slowed down. Malcolm threw up. Raul ran ahead so he wouldn't be late for school. Malcolm wiped his mouth on some tissue. I escorted him to the steps. He went to the nurse's station. I went straight to class."

"That's it?" The sheriff's glass eye twirled in its socket. His one good eye glittered. My stomach sank. I didn't think the sheriff believed me at all.

Granma put her arm around my shoulders. "Yo' heard my young'un tell yo' wha' happened. She's not a liar. Othah' kids I don' know 'bout. I just know my chile wouldn' lie."

The sheriff nodded. "Will you look at that? I forgot to turn the recorder back on."

"Do I have to repeat myself?"

He shook his head. "No, we got the important stuff. I'll do some more poking around. If you can prove that your brother got sick on the way to school, it would go a long way."

I shrugged my shoulders. "Ask Ms. Yolanda about the burned match she took from me. She'll show you." A sudden coldness numbed me. There wouldn't be a burnt match. It was gone when the school burned down. I was doomed. My stomach heaved. *Calm down, take a deep breath. Malcolm's vomit. Side of the road.* I struck my head.

"Wait, check out the side of the road. I'm pretty sure that pancake pieces and syrup are still there. It hasn't rained in a week."

"Now that's a thought. Not bad," the sheriff said. "Not bad at all. I best be on my way." He held out his hand. I stuck mine out. The sheriff shook it. "Ma'am, if you show me the way out, I best be on my way. Thank you. Good day to you all."

Granma marched out of the kitchen. The sheriff followed her. I stayed behind. I'd had enough of the sheriff to last me all day. I wanted to cry. My eyes twitched. My hands felt moist and cold. My throat ached. Malcolm walked in through the dining room door. "Is he done? What didja tell him."

"The truth."

I heard someone pound on the door. Granma and the sheriff strolled back into the kitchen. "I almost forgot," the sheriff said. "I forgot to ask you. Can you produce the tissue? I dug into my skirt pocket and handed him the crumbled tissue. His face lit up. He stepped closer to the chair and stooped down. The sheriff put his nose close to my blouse and skirt and sniffed. His nose wrinkled.

"Pshew! You smell of vomit." He walked up to Malcolm and held his head close to Malcolm's mouth. "Breathe out!"

Malcolm forced his breath. I saw the sheriff's face. It screwed up. He stepped backwards. "Whew, his breath is foul. It smells like a mixture of sour milk, stale pancake, and maple syrup. Don't you brush your teeth?"

Granma walked up to Malcolm. "Yo' believe 'em now?"

"I got my proof. I believe them. Now, how do I present this so that the rest of the school board, police department, and juvenile court believe them? Just a minute, Ma'am."

The sheriff took out his cell phone. He punched in a bunch of numbers and waited. I heard the phone ring. Ms. Yolanda's voice came through. The sheriff held the cell phone up to his mouth and spoke into it. His lips broke into a smile.

"Well, now, it seems that Ms. Yolanda confirms your story. She can produce the match for me. She's pretty sure that's what set off the sprinkler and the alarm. Of course that doesn't explain how the match got there in the first place, now does it?"

Granma spread out her arms as if to say, "It beats me." The sheriff left the kitchen. Granma followed him. I heard the front door open and then close. Granma came back alone into the kitchen. Her eyes twinkled. "The sheriff told me to tell yo' somethin'."

"What?"

"Always tell folks the truth, then yo' don' have t' make up tales."

"I did tell the truth."

"Not accordin' t' the sheriff. It's the smell tha' told 'em wha' he wantah t' know. Yo' and Malcolm are safe."

She winked at me.

Chapter Fourteen

Numbed, I walked to the phone, picked it up and dialed Raul's phone number. It rang and rang. I counted to ten and then threw the phone into its cradle. "I'm goin' t' Raul's. Be back 'fore yo' dinnah is put on the table."

I ran out of the kitchen, grabbed the front door knob, twisted it and opened the door. I ran smack into Raul. He stood on the stoop, with his abuelito and abuelita grouped behind him.

"Wha' are yo' doin' here?"

"Raul is here to apologize," Abuelita said. "When he came home early from school, we wanted to know why. He told us what happened."

"We told him that best friends don't act like that, no matter what," Abuelito said.

"You're innocent until you're proven guilty. That's why this country is so great," Abuelita added.

I looked at Raul. "We're even. I ran out on him when the fire sprinkler turned on."

His grandparents exchanged looks. Granma strolled into the hallway. Raul waved and smiled at her.

"Anna Mae! Yo' don' leave guests standin' in front of the door. Yo' 'nvite 'em int' the house. Where's yo' mannahs?"

Raul's lips twisted into a broad grin. "Want somethin' t' drink? Follah me."

I led him down the hallway and into the kitchen. He pushed past the door. "Neat! A swinging door."

"Yeah, can' get any bettah than that."

"Damn! They forgot."

"Wha'?"

"We brought dinner with us. A peace offering on our parts. I forgot to bring it in. I better go back out and bring it in before it cools off."

"I'll help."

"Yo' can hold the door open."

Raul left for the car. I followed him. He opened the rear door of the Cadillac and reached in. Backing out, I saw him lift out five cardboard boxes. He kicked up one knee and hoisted the boxes into both hands. I closed the car door behind him, and then hurried to the back door. He sailed through. I closed off the entrance behind us.

Raul managed to get the boxes to the table. He put them down. I scurried to the refrigerator and opened it.

"Smells like it's gonna rain."

"Hmm," Raul said.

He opened the first box and dug in.

"Here, take these. They belong in the ice box."

Raul unpacked the boxes and handed me the food his abuelita had prepared. When he was finished, Raul dug into his pocket. "Almost forgot, wanted to show you what Abuelito gave me when I was six years old. Hold on, I'd better get these in the refrigerator until our grandparents decide when it's time to eat," Raul said.

I crowded around him. "Wha' is it?"

"Yo' know tha' project we're doin' in Ms. Yolanda's class?"

"Yeah, it's due in Decembah."

Raul brought up his hand and opened it. Lying in his palm was a gold coin.

"Is it real?"

"Abuelito found it down by the river when he was a boy. Said it was a Confederate coin. Maybe it's one of the ones from Davis' treasure horde."

I stared at it. "Can I pick it up?"

"Be careful. It's a beauty."

On one side of the coin there was a picture of Jefferson Davis. I turned it over. On the other side the Confederate flag waved.

"I thought we could use it for show 'n tell when we do our oral reports."

The coin felt warm. It turned bright red and burned my fingers. I dropped it to the floor. It rolled six inches, wobbled and fell down flat. Its outer rim glowed. I gasped and crouched. Jefferson Davis' eyes moved. They held me in a tight embrace.

The room tilted. Around me, the walls grew black. A narrow tunnel forced me to look inward. I saw a bright, white light at its end and I moved towards it.

I hung in space, unaware of time passing. Rain stung my eyes, making them burn. I raised my hand and wiped away the splattering raindrops. They were cold. I shivered inside my oilskins. My feet hurt. My boots soaked through. I doubted if I could walk another step that cold May night.

We made camp while it was still daylight. The sudden downpour of rain forced us to put up our tents; otherwise, sleep would have been impossible.

Later that evening, an old man, dressed in a ragged gray uniform, stole into camp and approached me. He came to warn me that Federal troops were a half-day's ride away. I slipped him one silver ingot and bade him to leave.

He left without looking back. I went to the circled wagons and stared at their underbellies, hoping my ruse would work. Captain Micajah Clark sauntered up to me with a tin cup full of hot liquid. He held it between his fingers. I suspected it was chicory, since our real coffee was all gone. He offered me the cup. I declined.

"You won't make it to Abbeville with the gold if you travel with me. You'll make better time if I leave you. A spy came into camp and told me that Federal troops were not far off. I've decided to join my wife and children. Take this." I handed Captain Clark a hand-drawn map. "It gives you Indian trails and little-known roads to travel by so you can get to Abbeville without being seen. An old Methodist minister lives along the route. I made arrangements with him long ago, should I ever need his help."

Captain Clark studied the map and then pocketed it. He saluted and hurried away. I woke my darkie. He saddled my horse and packed what he could into the saddlebags. I told him to go with the captain, knowing he would use the slave well.

Around midnight, I cantered out of the encampment. I hoped that my leaving the wagon train would enable Captain Clark to get to the coast and beyond the reaches of the Union troops.

"Anna Mae?"

Rattling drums pounded my ears. The Protectoras stood in a clearing. Hay and prairie grass grew chest high. I inhaled. I could smell the sweetness of new-mown hay. Sunlight, pale and thin, reflected off the coin. I reached out, thinking a flame was burning, and snuffed it between my fingers like a lit candle.

The light vanished. My head trembled. All I wanted was to lie down and sleep. Sharp pains dug into the small of my back.

"Anna Mae?" I opened my eyes and stared into Raul's face. His lips moved. His voice sounded as if it was coming from far away. "It's raining and thundering. The rain is pelting the roof and ice pellets are bouncing off of it. I've never seen hail this early in the season. Yo' should see it. It's coming down in a slant. Granma Zora turned on the television to the Weather Channel."

Hail? Slanting rain? That wasn't what I feared. I smelled somethin' else, too: *greed!*

Chapter Fifteen

I covered my ears. The rattling hail unnerved me. "Where's Malcolm?"

"Is that all yo' can think 'bout? Malcolm's with yar granma and my grandparents in the living room."

"Thank God," I said. "I'm being hunted by Federal troops. At least my boy is safe with his mothahh."

Raul stared at me.

"Federal troops? Safe with his mothahh? Who are yo' talkin' 'bout now?"

I shook my head, trying to clear it. It seemed like two minds collided inside mine.

"Whatever," Raul grunted. He rubbed his stomach. "Let's remind our grandparents that it's time to eat. My stomach is runnin' on empty, even if theirs is not."

We left the kitchen and used my shortcut through the rear door. Cutting across the dining room, we sped into the living room to where our respective grandparents were sitting. Granma spoke up first.

"Raul's grandparents and I agree. All three of yo' should stick togethah and in one spot. Since yo' and Raul got tha' project t' do, we agreed tha' Raul should stick

133

'round for a bit. Tha' way yo' and him can get a runnin' start on it. Malcolm can help yo' too."

"Where's Raul gonna sleep?"

"With Malcolm," Granma said, "upstahs."

"I'm starved. When can we eat?" Raul asked.

Abuelito rose from the couch first. "We brought some food with us. It's in the car. Raul, come help me."

"Already brought it in," Raul said.

Abuelito smiled.

"Where did you stow it?" Abuelita asked, as she too rose from the couch. Granma followed. Malcolm remained inert. His snores sounded like pig snorts.

"I'm not sure whether he's asleep or not. Malcolm? Are you awake?" Malcolm didn't stir.

"Let me try." I stepped over him and kicked him. He groaned.

"Need some help?" Raul asked, his grin turning wicked. Without waiting for an answer, Raul sat down on top of Malcolm and tickled his sides.

"Stop that!" Malcolm yelled. "I'm up! I'm up!"

Raul stood up and stepped away. "It's time for supper."

"Set the table, Anna Mae."

While Granma, Miguel and Juanita sauntered into the kitchen, I stayed put in the living room with Raul and Malcolm. I hated setting the table. *That's girls' work,* everybody always said. *I believed in the equality of the sexes. Let Malcolm set the table.* For once Malcolm read my mind. "Who's gonna set the table?"

"Thanks for volunteerin'," I said as I winked at Raul, who grinned back at me. Malcolm glared. He left, muttering about big sisters and their lordly ways. I tuned him out.

"Wha's our next move?" Raul asked.

"Tha' coin yo' showed me. Is it still lyin' on the kitchen floor?"

"I forgot all about it!" Raul said and slapped his head. He leaped to his feet and dashed into the kitchen.

I heard Granma shout. Raul rushed out, his fist clenched. He grabbed me by the arm and dragged me toward the kitchen. "Yo' gotta see this!"

Malcolm followed behind us. I saw Abuelito standing in the middle of the kitchen, his arms held high above his head. Abuelita stood beside him with one of Granma's floral aprons held over her head. Granma sat on the floor, picking up golden coins from the floor. She threw them into a wash bucket that Poppa kept in the utility closet. "Quick, help me get these coins off the floor."

I stooped and picked up what I thought was a metal coin. When I brought it up to eye level, I noticed that part of the gold came away. *That can't be right,* I thought.

Raul stepped up and took the so-called coin from my hand. He pushed the loose part of gold away from the coin with his index finger. It fell off and spun down to the floor.

"It's candy, wrapped in gold foil," Raul said. He brought the coin up to his nose and sniffed. "Chocolate!" He popped it into his mouth and chewed.

"Lord have mercy!" Granma said as more candy flooded the kitchen floor. She stopped, scooping them into the bucket, and waited it out, along with Raul and me. Malcolm sat on the floor. He picked the candy coins up and threw them in the air to catch them again. His eyes glazed over, as if he couldn't believe our good fortune. I couldn't believe it either, except that Raul caught one or two of the coins and pocketed them. The rest of them he stripped and ate as he caught them.

Five minutes later, it was over. Miguel and Juanita hadn't stirred during the downpour. They now stretched and blinked. "Oh my!" Abuelita said. She stared dumbfoundedly at the floor. She lowered Granma's apron from her head. Abuelito lowered his arms. He looked at the floor and shook his head.

Raul shoved a dinette chair under Abeulito and he sat down hard on it. His eyes darted from Raul to Granma and then to me. "What happened? Where did these coins come from?"

Granma glanced at him. She shrugged her shoulders. "Ask 'em."

"I don't understand." Abuelita said.

A man's deep baritone laugh echoed through Granma's mouth. Abuelito clapped his hands over his ears. His lips formed a large "O." Abuelita clasped her arms across her stomach and leaned over. I heard her sob, but I didn't know whether she was crying or laughing. Granma covered her mouth, as if embarrassed like she had burped.

Raul stared at my granma. I thought his eyeballs would pop out of his head. Malcolm inched closer to me. He closed his eyes. I studied the ceiling tile and saw it; a disembodied black fist floated near the fluorescent lights, its fingers spread wide apart.

The apparition's fingers closed with a snap. "They wait, but can't wait forever. They use, but can't use forever. They take what is not theirs to take. They need, and their need is greater than ever."

The fist faded, like fog swallowed by sunlight. Someone tugged at my arm. I lowered my eyes. Malcolm's eyes were wide open. "The ghost spoke to yo'. Weren' you...scared?"

"What did it want?" Raul asked, his voice too loud and forced.

Granma smacked her hands together. "Anna Mae! Malcolm! Raul! Don' jus' stand there. Help me get the floor clean so we can eat dinnah!"

Granma handed us each a quart-size plastic bag. We got down on our hands and knees and picked up the coins from the floor. It only took a few seconds to pick up and stow the candy in the bags. When we were finished, Granma removed the containers Raul had placed in the refrigerator earlier. Everyone ate the Tex-Mex meal that Abuelita, Abuelito, and Raul had brought with them. The grandparents shooed us out of the kitchen. They cleaned up, all the time talking in hushed voices.

Even laying our ears against the kitchen door, we couldn't hear what they said. Defeated, we retreated to the shed. I closed the door. Malcolm sat on the bed with me. Raul sat on the floor.

"As long as you're sitting on the floor, pass me my backpack, will yo'?"

Raul scooted to the left and reached for it. He opened the flap and took out the history workbook. Handing me the book, I took it and flipped it open.

"What's that for?" Malcolm asked.

"Just curious 'bout somethin', tha's all." On page four, I found the brief section describing Jefferson Davis' lost Confederate gold. "From what I can see, the gold didn't travel a straight path to get out of Georgia. Listen to this. 'It went southwest to Sandersville and then headed north to Warthern. From Warthern, the wagons headed northeast toward Chennault Plantation. The route was planned to go on to Abbeville, South Carolina, and then to the coast, where a ship waited to take it to France.'

"The next paragraph says, 'The lost Confederate gold was claimed by many people: African Americans, Confederate cabinet members, Union troops and Confederate troops, a Methodist minister, the Mumfords, and the Pinkerton Detective Agency. Rumors stated that buried coins could be found in Wilkes, Washington, and Lincolnton Counties and Warthen's, if one knew where to look.'"

"Is tha' it, or is there more?"

I scanned the rest of the page until I saw a bit of information removed from the rest of the text. It was centered under a photograph of Jefferson Davis as a separate column on the right hand side of the page.

"'In eighteen hundred and sixty-four, when Jefferson Davis needed money to support his cause, he took a loan from the French government with the understanding that whether the South won or lost The War Between the States, in ten years the South would pay back the loan, with interest.'"

"Does that mean if we find the gold we have to give it back to France?"

"I don't think so. The book says that the treasure was assembled from different places. A private bank in Virginia claims it was worth two hundred and fifty thousand dollars. Another bank in Richmond says it's worth five hundred thousand dollars. The money was to pay Confederate troops who were fighting for the cause. Jefferson Davis claimed that he carried thirty-five thousand dollars until he gave ten thousand dollars of it to C.S. Captain Micajah Clark.

"Captain Clark took the ten thousand dollars with him to Florida, but he gave the remaining twenty thousand dollars to Mrs. Davis."

"My head hurts. How many people are claiming a share of the money if and when it's found?" Malcolm asked.

"It 'pends," I said.

"There's got to be a better way to figure this mess out," Raul said.

"We need t' get t' the library, use their computers and print out the information. Malcolm, brin' yo' notebook with yo'. We'll need t' write the information down. Next, we need t' find an old map of Georgia tha' was used durin' The War Between the States. We can trace the route tha' Jefferson Davis and the wagon train took t' 'scape from the Yankee soldiers. We can use a current map of Georgia and see if we can find the same roads that Davis and the wagon train used."

"Don't forget that Davis and the wagon train split up. Davis went further south, but the wagon train headed north upon his instructions," Raul added.

"I haven't forgotten. We can follow the same road and perhaps find the lost gold."

"That would be nice," Raul said.

"When do we go to the library?" Malcolm asked.

"We'll go now. The library doesn't close until nine o'clock, and it's not even seven. Let's ask Granma if she'll drive us," I said.

"If not, I'm sure Abuelito would do it. A way for 'em to keep an eye on all of us."

I placed the workbook on the bed and got to my feet. Raul rose from the floor. Malcolm bounced off the bed. We dashed out of the shed and into the kitchen. The grandparents sat at the table, drinking coffee.

"You're in a hurry," Abuelito said.

"Can yo' take us t' the library? We need t' do some research for our project."

Granma put down her coffee cup. "I might. Wha' 'bout y'all? Wanna join us?"

Abuelito checked his watch. "As long as Juanita and I can get home by nine. We like watching reruns of 'The Waltons.'"

"I'll get my notebook," Malcolm said. He hurried out of the kitchen and ran into the hallway. I heard him double-step up the stairs. I went into the shed and retrieved my raincoat. I saw that Granma had the beach umbrella out when I returned to the kitchen. I heard Malcolm jump down each step, doing his happy walk. Like me, he wore a yellow slicker with a detachable hood.

We met up at the front door. Abuelito took Granma's umbrella. He escorted his wife to the Cadillac that was parked out in the driveway. He came back for Granma and Raul. Malcolm and I followed, protected in our raingear. Granma climbed into the back seat. Malcolm slid in next to her. I went to the other side of the car, opened the door and stuffed myself in. Raul sat up in front with his grandparents.

The ride didn't take long. The lights were still on, and the doors were open. Abuelito drove up to the front entrance. I opened the rear door and stepped out first. Malcolm slid out next, followed by Granma. Raul stepped out of the front seat, holding Granma's umbrella. He opened it, and Abuelita slid out and stood up under the umbrella with Raul. Abuelito went to park the car. We trooped inside. Granma and Abuelita left us and strolled to the magazine rack.

We walked to the reference desk. I rummaged through my slicker pocket and found my library card. I showed it to the librarian. He turned on the third computer. Raul, Malcolm, and I walked over to it. I sat down. Raul and Malcolm crowded behind me.

I pushed ENTER. The screen cleared to TOPIC.

"Put in War Between the States," Malcolm said.

"We need key words. Type in: Jefferson Davis, lost Confederate gold, and eighteen hundred and sixty-five," Raul suggested.

I typed in all the words, and pushed ENTER. The screen filled with a list of websites. I clicked the one on the third line down. The screen filled with information about

Jefferson Davis and his gold. "The Mystery of the Lost Confederate Gold. According to what source you read, the lost Confederate gold of Jefferson Davis was an enormous sum. In one statement, a bank in Virginia declared that it was worth two hundred and fifty thousand dollars. The bank claimed the funds were taken out by Jefferson Davis and were stowed aboard wagon trains in his flight from the Yankees.

"Another source states that approximately five hundred thousand dollars was taken from a bank in Richmond, Virginia and was to pay all the fighting troops of the Confederacy.

"A third source states that the lost Confederate gold consisted of gold coins, silver ingots, and paper Confederate money.

"Of course, we may never know what the exact amount was or who the money was intended for. It doesn't matter, because the lure of this lost Confederate gold has driven people over the past century to look for it all over the northeastern part of Georgia. At any one time, motorists can see respectable people digging holes while clutching so-called authenticated gold maps sold in Lincolnton, Wilkes, and Washington counties.

"Many of the older families claim that the gold is still buried. Go look after heavy rainstorms and find the golden coins; they're exposed as the rain washes the dirt away. Several coins were found during the early part of the twentieth century, but nothing since then."

"Is that it?" Malcolm asked.

"They've got a picture of Jefferson Davis and a history of Davis' flight toward the coast."

"Does it show a map?" Raul asked.

"We can go to 'Journey-Now' for the current Georgia roads. I need one from eighteen hundred and sixty-five."

"Type in the key words and let's see what turns up," Raul said.

I typed in "Map, Georgia, eighteen hundred and sixty-five, and Northeastern." The screen flashed up a list of websites, including several universities, bookstores, libraries, and commercial map-sellers.

"Let's start here," I said as I clicked on one of the universities. It took me to its web page. I read "Maps" first. Underneath were the names of all the wars in America. I found the Civil War and clicked on it. A huge list of map titles appeared on the screen. I read down the screen and stopped at Northeastern Georgia, eighteen hundred and sixty-five, including counties, back roads, and major cities.

I felt Raul's chin resting on my left shoulder. His warmth heated my chilled body. "Click on that one," he said, pointing.

I looked at the year, and nodded. I clicked on that one particular area, watched as the map filled the page, and then shrank to a smaller picture.

"Click on the zoom button so we can enlarge it."

I clicked on it. The map became bigger. "Think about some of the clues we got from the disembodied black fist, the alphabet soup, and those scraps of paper."

"Sandersville," Raul said into my ear. His lips tickled. "That's where Davis split up with the wagon train."

"Good. Chennault Plantation is one of the sentences that was written on the blackboard with the floating chalk. What's next?"

"I just remember what the window told us, Anna Mae Botts. I really didn't see all of the clues," Malcolm said.

"What else? Davis owes money. That's one of them. Two black soldiers driving a wagon train, and they bury money. Hmm. Ask *Mary Anne*. We might as well," I said.

I printed the map page out, then I went back and printed the page of information I had found about the lost gold. Next I typed in "Mary Anne" and then stopped. "We need more information."

"Put in 'Chennault Plantation, buried Confederate gold,' and see what happens," Raul said.

I typed in 'Chennault Plantation, buried Confederate gold' and clicked. The screen showed up a list of four web sites. I chose the second one on a hunch. The page appeared. Right in front of my face appeared these words: "Eighteen hundred sixty-five, Mr. Dionysius Chennault, a Methodist Minister and elderly planter, was owner of Chennault Plantation. His daughter, Mary Anne, when asked by treasure seekers where it was buried, told people to look between Lincolnton and Washington Counties. Some are hidden in swamps. Others are buried in the ground. The rest of it, the Yankees took, although this writer believes that some of the gold is buried near the Apalachee and Oconee Rivers."

"Print that out," Malcolm said.

"I am. We need all the information we can get, plus what we can take from the clues that were given to us."

"Do you think we have enough?" Raul asked.

"I believe so. We can always come back on Saturday if we need more."

"If you say so..." Raul let his voice trail off.

"Malcolm, go tell Granma we're ready to leave."

Malcolm trotted off as if Confederate troops were chasing him. Granma appeared in two shakes of a lamb's tail.. "Yo' got wha' yo' wanted?"

"Yes."

"Good. Let me get Abuelita. Miguel stayed in the car. Let's all walk out t' the car. I don' want 'em t' make an extra trip for us. 'Sides, the rain stopped. I don't see it fallin'."

Raul fetched Abuelita, while Malcolm, Granma and I waited at the entrance. Granma stared at my hands. "Do yo' have everythin'?"

I stared at Raul, and then at Malcolm. I hit myself. "The print-outs! I forgot them." I ran back to computer three. The paper sagged on the floor. The librarian scowled and pointed. I picked up the paper from the floor and folded it. At the printer, I tore it off and retreated, probably much like Jefferson Davis did with his gold.

Chapter Sixteen

When we arrived home, Abuelito drove up into the driveway. He left the motor running while he escorted Granma to our front door. Malcolm, Raul, and I slid out of our respective seats, and ran up the sidewalk. Granma unlocked the door. Raul, Malcolm, and I rushed past her, into the house.

We hurried to the kitchen and pulled out three chairs. I thumped the printed paper on the table. All three of us sat down and scooched our chairs up closer to the table.

"Anyone want lemonade?" Malcolm asked.

"Nothin' for me," I said. Raul shook his head.

Malcolm lunged at the cabinet. With glass in hand he reached the sink and turned on the faucet. The water gushed from the pipes, distracting me. He let it run for several minutes before he filled his glass and came back. Raul pulled the paper toward him and unfolded it. He separated the map of Georgia from the rest of the information.

"Malcolm, go t' Poppa's study and get his current map of Georgia. It's in the middle drawer of his desk."

Scowling, Malcolm got up for the third time. He left the kitchen. Sometimes, he was a pain in the ass. Malcolm came back seconds later with Poppa's Georgia map. Raul snatched it from Malcolm's hand. I leaned over and grabbed it from Raul. I spread it flat on the table and smoothed out all the creases.

"We need a magnifying glass," Raul said.

"I'll get it. I'm still standing." Malcolm said.

He left the kitchen a second time. I got up and went to the refrigerator and took out the pitcher of lemonade. I dumped the rest of the water in the sink and filled Raul's glass with lemonade. I went to the pantry and took out the cookie tin. Placing it on the table, I pulled Malcolm's chair out for him. Raul and I studied Poppa's map while we waited for Malcolm.

Malcolm shoved open the door. He held the magnifying glass up in front of him. "Here!" he said and handed the glass to Raul, who passed it over to me.

"Thanks, Anna Mae!" Malcolm said as he spied the lemonade and cookie tin. He sat in the chair with one leg folded underneath the other one. He reached for the tin, removed the lid, and dug in. I studied the Northeastern section of the map.

I found Lowery and pointed to it. Raul and Malcolm grinned and punched each other in the shoulder. Male bonding, I supposed, and I kept looking. Finding Bradford Road, I followed it southeast to Georgia 44. Georgia 44 led straight to Chennault Plantation. It was north of Lincolnton. From the plantation, I followed route Georgia 44. It changed into Georgia 80. Georgia 80 became Georgia 16. Georgia 16 took me straight to Sandersville.

The road twisted and turned. It passed through several towns: Washington, Warrenton, and Warthen. That's when I stopped. Why did Warthen sound so familiar?

"I found Sandersville. Let's put an X by each place so we don't lose them. It will make it easier when we compare maps and try to find the exact routes that Jefferson Davis and the wagon trains took."

Malcolm was out of his chair before I could ask. He shoved the swinging door and ran. Malcolm returned with all of Poppa's magic markers. He gave me the yellow highlighter first. I marked Lowery, Chennault Plantation, Warrenton, and Sandersville with it. "What other names did we find?"

"Warthen," Raul said. "Both Davis and the wagon trains went that way."

"Aha! I see the connection." I bent over the map and found Warthen on Georgia 16, north of Sandersville. "Give me the blue marker."

Malcolm handed it over. I marked Warthen in blue. What's next?"

Raul's eyebrows pinched together. He pulled the printed paper toward him. Malcolm licked his lips, and finished his lemonade in one gulp. He poured himself another glass and sat back with a sigh.

Raul drummed his fingers on the table. He kept retracing the route with his forefinger. Suddenly he stopped drumming. "I found Gibson."

"Get your fat finger out of the way so I can see it too. Hand me the red marker, Malcolm."

Malcolm straightened up and handed me the red marker. Raul moved his finger a fraction. I saw Gibson. It was one of the towns mentioned on the eighteen hundred and sixty-five map of Washington County.

"Are there any more cities, roads, or counties that we can find on this map?"

"You're including counties too? Sparta! Why didn't you say so?"

Raul snorted. "Let me see if I can find the counties. We live in Wilkes County. Chennault Plantation is in Lincoln County."

"Two places to search. Where else?"

"Dublin's further south than Sandersville on Georgia 57. See?" Raul said.

Fidgeting, I kept stabbing the map with one end of a marker. Don't ask me why I felt so uncomfortable. Impatient, I wanted to find it now, not later. I was like a cat on a hot tin roof. I guess finding historical information matching the myths and stories that we'd found was unnerving me. It began to sink in. The lost Confederate gold was real, and not just a story or rumor.

"What's next?" Malcolm asked.

Raul looked up from the map, waiting for me to answer. I closed my eyes and saw nothing. I heard no sounds, smelled no scents, and received no further clues. "What about swamps? Are there any nearby?"

Raul bent over the map "Oconee Swamp. It must connect to the river. The river is somewhere around here. Damn! I can't find it."

"Raul, let's place the eighteen hundred and sixty-five map of Northeastern Georgia next to Poppa's map. Let's see if we can find similar names of the cities, counties, roads, and rivers. We can match them."

Raul put the older map side by side with Poppa's. He used the magnifying glass and with his forefinger traced the routes, cities, and counties we'd already mentioned. He pointed to the places where Jefferson Davis and the wagon trains might have passed through.

We found several names that matched. The spelling sometimes threw us off because it had changed over the years. The land, too, had changed since the War Between the States and boundary lines had shifted during that one hundred and thirty year period.

"Let's sort through the information and review the clues we've received from various sources—scraps of paper, the disembodied black fist, alphabet soup, frosted windows, and the library—and try to make some sense from it."

"It's gonna take all night," Malcolm groaned.

"Don' do me any favors. Go t' bed if yo' want, but I'm stayin' put. Raul, wha' 'bout yo'? Goin' or stayin'?"

"Miss all of this? Not on yo' sweet life, Sis. I'm stayin' put," Malcolm said.

"As long as yo' stayin', be a dear and get me a pad and pen from Poppa's study. Thanks Malcolm, yo' one in a zillion."

"If I haveta," Malcolm said as he dashed out of the kitchen.

"Bossy, aren't you? Sure glad yo' not my sistah."

I grinned. "Me too."

Malcolm returned with three pens and three lined legal-size pads. I blew him a kiss. He dodged it, but handed the stuff to me.

"Raul, yo' write. Malcolm, yo' help us think. Got t' get the clues down in ordah, and then we can go t' bed."

I gave the pens and pads to Raul. Malcolm's eyes were half-closed, his lips pressed together. I glanced at Raul. He bit the tip of one of the pens. His fingers lay flat on the table. I glanced up to the ceiling and waited. The kitchen was still.

Raul broke the silence first. "This is what we know." Malcolm and I jerked our heads up. "The black fist spoke to us first. He dropped the paper clues to us. 'Find the gold. Find the house where Davis lost it.' We now know that the gold belonged to Jefferson Davis. The gold was lost—at Chennault Plantation in Lincoln County, Georgia."

I watched as Raul wrote that down and thought. "The next set of clues came from our classroom that morning."

"Three things were written on the blackboard. The first two were, 'Send her home. The gold isn't here.' The school caught fire and burned down. We were sent home. Another set of clues came true."

Raul took up where I left off. "The second sentence tells us no gold was buried in Lowery, although the material at the library says different."

"Write all tha' down, Raul. We'll need it for latah. The next sentences gave us another clue."Go to Chennault Plantation. The gold is buried there. Davis owes money.' The plantation is a given. The gold being buried there is new. Davis owes money."

"French gold, that's the money Davis owes." Raul said

I repeated what Raul stated. "The French loaned ten million dollars to Davis, whether he won or lost the war."

"It never got there," Malcolm said.

"Someone got to it first," I said.

"Depending on who you believe or what you read," Raul added.

"Let's see. The fire alarm went off without reason. Our class moved to the gym. I found a burned match under my desk and gave it to Ms. Yolanda. After lunch we held class in the auditorium, where I had a vision."

"Still not tellin' me everythin'. It's not fair," Malcolm said, stamping his feet under the table.

"I'm sorry." I wasn't sorry at all, although I would never tell Malcolm that.

"Let's find tha' gold. Visions can' always be shared and 'sides, they're not important. Wha's next? The alphabet soup letter clues appeared. Raul, do yo' remembah any of the words tha' the noodle letters spelled?"

Raul cocked his head. "*FRENCH GOLD*. Then, came *BURIED COINS. FEDERAL TROOPS. ASK MARY ANNE. WARTHEN, GA. BUMFORD GOLD*."

"Mary Ann! I met her in the vision, along with the gold coins her father buried off the plantation. He planted several coins in the barn to throw off the Union Major and his soldiers. Warthen, Georgia is one of the places where the gold traveled through. Bumford gold. I don' know wha' t' make of tha' one."

Raul took up my clue deductions. "We know where Warthen is because it's marked on the map. What I find funny is that Warthen isn't mentioned in any of the information that we found at the library."

"Did it exist in Jeff Davis' time?" Malcolm asked.

Raul stared. "Did yo' vision show yo' how them Yankees knew about the gold shipment? Or even where to find the wagon trains?"

"My vision didn' say. We might have t' go back t' the library for tha'," I said.

"And Bumford? It don't sound like a person's name. Maybe, it's not spelled right, or spelled wrong on purpose."

Raul and I glanced at him. Malcolm had a point. "Bumford" sounded like a made-up name. That set me to thinking. "I guess we'll need t' get back t' the library tomorrow mornin' 'fore we leave for Chennault. There are t' many unanswered clues."

"What's next? My fingers are getting tired," Raul said.

I looked hard at him. "Yo' want t' quit now?"

"No!" both Raul and Malcolm shouted together.

"Let's finish up. Anythin' happen aftah the noodle words?"

"Pinkerton Agency."

Chapter Seventeen

"Who said that?" Malcolm asked.

I checked the ceiling. I studied the floor. A slight chill rounded my shoulders, then it was gone. Silence. A stillness settled in the room. Raul pushed his chair away from the table, causing a sudden squeak. Malcolm farted. I held my nose. We all laughed.

"What does the Pinkerton Agency have to do with Jefferson Davis' gold?" Raul asked. "That clue doesn't make any sense to me."

Malcolm's head bobbed against his chest. "He's out cold," I said.

"Let's finish up and get to bed," Raul said. He finished writing as he stood. The pen dropped from his fingers. Raul rubbed them with his left hand. I stared at my own fingers and remembered how cramped and stiff they were after holding soaked leather reins for hours. Jefferson Davis popped into my mind. I saw in the wagons. Ex-slaves drove those wagons. I wondered how they felt about helping a man who kept them enslaved and were now part of his retreat to freedom.

"The southern Cabinet members were involved too. We know that Confederate and Yankee troops stole the gold. Perhaps we can find some other names at the library."

"Let's call it quits. Malcolm's down for the count. I'm 'most there, and so should yo' be if yo' had any sense. If I keep yawnin' like this, I'll split in two."

Raul shook Malcolm's shoulders. He awoke with a yawn and a stretch. I reached and picked up the two maps, the printed paper, and the pad and pens from the table. After Malcolm and Raul stumbled out of the kitchen it was too quiet. The kitchen door swooshed. Granma stood dressed in her yellow cotton bathrobe and ballerina slippers.

"I'm off t' bed. It's close t' midnight. When did Raul's grandparents leave?"

"'Bout an hour ago. They plan t' come with us when we look for gold. Miguel thought we might need their help, should we find it."

I gritted my teeth. "This is our treasure hunt. I don' want 'em t' tag 'long. Bad 'nough we need yar help."

"Wha's wrong with yo', chile. Yar gonna need their help should y'all find the gold. Tha' stuff is heavy, not like the coins we use t'day. 'Sides, yo' and Malcolm are still 'spects in the school fire. My grannie use t' say 'Don' look a gift horse in the mouth.'"

"Okay," I shouted. "Okay! Yo' win. All of yo'. I just want yo' t' know that this is Raul's and my school project. I don' want Ms. Yolanda 'cusin' us of cheatin', tha's all."

"Don' worry, chile. I'm just the escort, as yo' Momma use t' say when I went with her on dates with yo' Poppa." She grinned.

I felt like Judas must've felt after betraying Jesus. "All right, have it yar way. I'm wrong, yar right. Does tha' make yo' feel bettah?"

"Yes, lots bettah. Yo' feel bettah t', when yo' and Raul find tha' gold. Miguel will help y'all carry it t' the car. Malcolm will want t' help t', knowin' Malcolm."

"Yo' win! Tomorrow mornin' I'll tell 'em and let 'em know tha' we've got company. Tha' save Raul from tellin' me 'I tole yo' so.' Are we goin' in Poppa's station wagon?"

"I can drive it," Granma said.

"Wha' 'bout the Garcias? They comin' with us?'"

"They're takin' their Cadillac. Miguel feels tha' the station wagon can' carry t' much weight. I 'spect he means Abuelita's and his weight. 'Tween yo', Malcolm, Raul, and me, our total weight is 'round four hundred pounds. Too much for the station wagon t' carry. Tha's anothahh reason why Abuelito and Abuelita are comin' in their Cadillac."

"Where will they meet us?"

"Parked on the side of the road, Georgia 44. We don' want t' many people sniffin' 'round. Findin' the gold on the plantation will cause 'nough of a stir."

Granma's eyes twinkled. "Weren' yo' goin' t' bed?"

I yawned. "Night, Granma." I plodded out of the kitchen, through the bedroom, and into the shed. A bare bulb lit the room. By my bed, a shadow loomed. It was the Protectora's.

Chapter Eighteen

Friday

I got out of bed the next morning and looked out the window. It was still raining. It came down in sheets. Dressing in three-quarter length crinkle cotton pants and a matching red tee shirt, I walked into the kitchen. At one end of the table sat Granma, drinking her morning coffee. She was dressed in an old pair of dungarees and Poppa's castoff camouflage shirt. No one else was up.

"Want breakfast?"

"Cereal, milk and juice, please."

Granma put her cup on the table and got up from the chair. She walked to the refrigerator and took out a carton of milk and orange juice. I went to the pantry and took the "O-So-Fine" box from the shelf. Granma set the two cartons on the table with a glass, bowl, and a soup spoon. She sat down and finished drinking her coffee.

I poured the cereal into the bowl. Two strips of paper tumbled out of the box and landed on top of the flakes.

We both stared at my cereal bowl. I picked up the papers, shook cereal dust from them and placed them flat on the table. Granma's eyes remained glued on the scraps.

"Are yo' goin' t' share?"

I picked up one and read it aloud. "I can no longer wait. Find me!"

Granma squirmed. She rolled her eyes. "Wha' 'bout the othahh one? Wha' does it say?"

I picked up the other one from the table. "Find it now while their attention is elsewhere." For some reason, I turned the paper over. It read, "Wait too long and they'll claim it!"

"Sounds like a warnin'," I said.

"It does, doesn' it?"

Granma's lips parted. She whistled. I gazed at her. How could Granma do that? She was close to 70. Granmas don' whistle. She played with her coffee cup, and then leaned over the table. In a falsetto voice Granma said, "Miguel and Juanita, Raul and Malcolm, and Zora make five. Where goes the sixth? Is she aware? Find the bags that Davis borrowed before they disappear from view altogether."

I froze.

Granma wasn't finished. "The Protectora knows and sees all. Read the clues. Use your head. Focus. Understand. Mark them well. Once used and freely given, no longer can we spell it out. Heed us well, Anna Mae, and take the route that Davis used. Step aside or have another find the gold; all is lost and enslaved you will become again."

She lowered her voice. A mere whisper, but still in falsetto, one last clue the Protectora gave me. "Beware of false visions. They don't always speak truth."

Malcolm and Raul charged into the kitchen. They were dressed alike in worn and ragged jeans and olive drab tee shirts. Malcolm hiccupped. "G-g-g-ood morning. Let's eat and then split."

"You got it wrong, Malcolm. We can eat in the car and split at the same time," Raul said.

"Yo've got it wron', both of yo'," Granma threw in. "First thin's first. Eat. Pens. Pads. Papah. Roads y'all want t' go on."

"So eat," I said. "I'll get the stuff and show Granma the roads, cities, and counties we marked. Abuelito and Abuelita can follow behind us once we meet up. Not a big deal, Granma. Come on, yo' two, get movin'. We don' got all day, yo' know?"

"Lord have mercy! T' think I would take advice from a twelve-year-old young'un."

Malcolm stopped dead in his tracks. "Is Granma comin' with us?"

"Yar goin' t' drive the *station wagon*?"

Malcolm scowled at me. He pulled his lips back like a wild dog. "I've been thinkin', wha' do I get outta this?"

"Goin' on a treasure hunt and findin' gold. Wha' else?"

"Do I get some of it...if we find any? I'm part of the team, right?"

Raul threw his arm around Malcolm's shoulders. "We couldn' do it without yo'."

Malcolm beamed. I sighed in relief. Sometimes brothers were such a pain. Buying him off was a good idea though. Had to keep that in mind next time he proved to be a bigger pain than he was worth. Granma got up from the table and disappeared into the guest bedroom. She returned, wearing a huge yellow slicker poncho.

"Y'all need slickers. It's rainin' cats and dogs out there. Malcolm, I know tha' yo've got anothahh one upstairs. Go get it. Anna Mae, yo' can use the umbrella if yo' want."

While Malcolm ran back upstairs, Granma poured herself another cup of coffee. Raul wolfed down a bowl of cereal and gulped one glass of orange juice and milk in quick succession. I shuddered. Raul grinned. "It all mixes together in my stomach. No harm done."

How yucky, I thought, but it was his stomach, not mine. I took the umbrella from the stand in the hallway and joined Granma back in the kitchen. Malcolm ran to the kitchen. He had my backpack with him. "I stuffed everythin' in there. Hope yo' don' mind."

"Malcolm, yar a genius," I said.

He beamed.

Granma finished drinking her second cup of coffee. Raul finally showed up. He wore an old slicker of Malcolm's. It barely fit him, but enough of him was covered so that he wouldn't get too wet.

"Everyone here and accounted for?" I asked.

We left by the shed's rear door. It led straight to the garage. Granma waited until we were all out of the house, then she locked the door and set the alarm. Raul and Malcolm had already settled in the station wagon. It had seen better days. Poppa swore it would be the last car a thief would steal. The bumper sagged. The rear window sported a crack from a stone thrown up by a garbage truck. The tires bulged and all four hubcaps disappeared years ago. Scratches, dents, rust, and the trunk tied down with chicken wire, I agreed with Poppa. No one in their right mind would steal *his* car.

I saw that the front seat was vacant. Good! That meant they knew I was the key to unraveling the clues.

Granma strode to the station wagon and opened its door. It creaked. She climbed in. I went around to the right side and joined her. Malcolm handed me the backpack. "Seatbelts on?" Malcolm sang out.

I buckled my seatbelt. Granma reached overhead to the sun visor and pushed the button on the garage door opener. The door clacked and groaned as it lifted. Granma backed the station wagon down the driveway, and out into the street. She pushed the garage door opener button again and the door rolled with moans to shut.

Granma drove the station wagon as if she carried eggs and crystal inside. "Where to?"

"The library first," I said.

She made a U turn and drove toward the library. We arrived at nine-thirty. The head librarian opened the entrance door. I scooted in first, followed by Raul, Malcolm, and Granma. I made a beeline to the computer. Raul and Malcolm followed at my heels. Granma settled herself on one of the couches and closed her eyes.

Turning on the computer, I waited for the screen to appear with the instructions. For my first entry, I typed in the key words, "Pinkerton Agency, eighteen hundred and sixty-five." The screen went blank and then filled with several pages of URL website information. I scanned the list until I found one site that might contain the information we needed. Raul and Malcolm breathed down my neck their hot breaths tickling my nape hairs.

"Hey, check this out. *Legends of Lost Gold*. It states here that the Chennault Family was taken to Washington, D.C. where they were under intensive interrogation by Pinkerton's men to find out where the gold was hidden. The family members didn't tell their tormentors a word. Pinkerton's was ordered to release the Chennaults after a few weeks. They went back to Georgia and weren't harassed again by the Federal authorities."

"One done. Now we know why the Pinkerton Agency was involved. And the Southern cabinet members, where do they fit in?" Raul asked.

"Don't forget to print it out," Malcolm reminded me.

I printed the first screen, then typed in new key words: "Southern Cabinet Members."

"Try Jefferson Davis' Cabinet members and see what the computer finds," Raul said.

"Hmm, 'The Lore of Rebel Gold. Jefferson Davis and his Cabinet fled Richmond on April second, eighteen hundred and sixty-five.' It says that Jefferson Davis carried with them approximately five hundred thousand dollars in specie, silver bricks and gold ingots. 'The bulk of the treasure was given to them by England in addition to other monies taken from a Richmond bank that totaled two hundred thousand dollars.'"

"What' specie?" Malcolm asked.

Raul and I exchanged looks. I marched to the dictionary in the Reference Section and looked up the word. "Specie" means "money in coin." *That's helpful*, I thought as I walked back to the computer. When I drew closer, I told them, "The dictionary states the specie means 'money in coin.' The money that Jefferson Davis carried was 'five hundred thousand dollars in coins.'"

"Pretty heavy stuff to put in a wagon, don' yo' think? He wouldn't carry it in his pockets now, would he?" Malcolm said.

Raul and I exchanged looks. I giggled. "Malcolm, yo' made the understatement of the year."

I pressed the printer key. The paper typed the information we needed for our project and our treasure hunt.

Raul scratched his head. "Wha' does England have t' do with Jefferson Davis—or his Cabinet, for tha' mattah? Does the website say anythin' else?" Raul asked.

"Wait! There's a side note. 'Before Davis dismissed his Cabinet, he gave them an enormous amount of money to be split equally. He told each member that they were to spend the money as they saw fit. Davis fled Richmond and tried outrunning the Federal troops, but he wasn't fast enough.'"

"I guess that answers that. Wha' 'bout them Yankees who were chasin' 'em? Does it give a name?"

I scanned the rest of the website. It said zip about the Yankees and gave no names. I entered new key words: "Yankee troops, Rebel Gold, eighteen hundred and sixty-five." A whole page appeared. I studied the list and picked one. The site gave names, dates, places, and a lot more.

"Whoo hee! Look at this. Pay dirt! It's like a roll call of who's who in the Confederate army—C.S. Capt. Micajah Clark, U.S. Army Captain Lot Abraham, and C.S. Brig. Gen. Alexander, Captain Parker of the Navy."

Raul bit his lip. "All those *trusted* officers, and they still failed to get the money to the coast."

Granma appeared out of nowhere. "Find wha' y'all were lookin' for?"

"Almost," I said.

"Who's missin'?"

"Bumford," Malcolm said.

"Bumford? Name sounds familiar. Yo' don' mean Mumford, do yo'?"

"Don' know. The name given was Bumford."

"Now Mumford, tha's an old southern family. They used t' live near Waynesville on a plantation they built again aftah the war. Mr. Mumford claimed he was given money by Jefferson Davis, when he let the southern Cabinet go. The stories 'bout tha' money was told all ovah the place. It was given t' students who couldn' 'ford t' go t' college. I reckon tha' money is still given t' needy students today."

We walked out of the library. It had stopped raining. We walked to the station wagon, armed with our new information. My backpack bulged.

"Wha' our next stop?" Granma asked.

"Chennault Plantation," I said.

"'Fore we start, I want t' make sure y'all get the stuff I brought with me." Granma handed out brown paper lunch bags. I peeked inside. A pint carton of milk, a chocolate bar, a wrapped sandwich in aluminum, and an apple was our lunch.

"Three books for Malcolm so he won' get bored. Magnifying glass, markers—and oh yes, a flashlight, just in case."

I hauled my backpack to my lap and untied the flap. I stuck my hand in and came out with our two Georgia maps—the old and the new. I lay them on my lap. I dug into the bag and withdrew two pens and the pad. The printouts were stuck in between the pad's lined yellow pages. "

Granma watched me. "Yo' got everythin'?"

"I'm okay," I said.

Granma took the map off my lap and unfolded it. She spread it across the steering wheel. Wetting her finger, she pointed on the map next to Lowry. I blinked. *Maybe it was a good idea that Granma came along after all.* I waited for her next instructions.

"Here's where we'll start," she said as I leaned sideways and stared. Granma's finger shot straight up the road to Chennault Plantation. She wasn't even paying attention as she spoke. "We go southeast on Bradford Road, cross 132 toward Lowery Road, then it turns into Georgia 44.

"We continue on Georgia 44. It takes us directly t' the city of Chennault."

Granma refolded the map and gave it back to me. "Everyone ready?"

A chorus of "yeses" came from Raul, Malcolm, and me. She started the engine. It sputtered, backfired, and off we went.

Sixteen minutes later, we arrived in the city of Chennault. "Yo' and Raul should go t' the real estate office and get permission t' dig on tha' property. We don' want any trouble with the law. The real estate buildin' is a block down this road. We'll park in front while y'all go in and ask. Malcolm will stay in the station wagon with me. Less is more."

I paused before opening the door. "Granma, why is a realtor sellin' Chennault Plantation, and not its ownah?"

"When a plantation like Chennault changes hands, the owner wants someone else t' represent 'em. They hire an agent." She coughed as if arranging her thoughts. "Sometimes the cost of a plantation is t' much t' bear for the owner. The house is bought by a bank, or in this case, by the county. I understand from my sources tha' the Lincoln County Development Authority is handlin' the house and land. They wanted an agent to find a buyer for 'em."

"The house is registered as a national historical monument, and is no longer privately owned?" Raul asked.

"They did tha' t' protect the buildin' from fallin' down and the land divided int' sections. It keeps people from destroyin' the house or refurbishin' it in such a manna tha' it would take away from its old southern charm. Chennault Plantation is a working plantation, which means tha' the public is invited in t' learn 'bout its past and its place in southern history."

The parking lot was empty in front of the real estate office. Raul and I slid out of the station wagon and walked into the office. Our raincoats dripped on the floor.

A woman looked up from a pile of papers. "Can I help you?" she drawled.

"We need your permission to walk around Chennault Plantation. We're doing a history project for school," I said.

"How nice. Did you hear that, Franklin? They're doing a history project."

"My granma says I need written permission to walk on the grounds."

"You're not going to dig up anything, are you?" the woman asked.

"Not that you'll find anything," Franklin said, "There's nothing there for you to find."

"If you do find something," the woman realtor said, "tell me and we'll announce it in the local *Realtor News*. The find of the century," Franklin laughed.

"Don't pay any attention to him. Everyone has dug on that old plantation, and nobody's ever found nothing," the woman agent said.

"We just want to take a look and dig a hole or two just for the heck of it," Raul said.

"I know exactly what you want." She giggled. "You can't go into the house. It's locked, but you can look through the windows. There are no drapes, so you can see a lot. You have our permission to walk on the property and even dig your holes. Just make sure you fill them so no one trips or falls in." She giggled harder. "Allow me to write out your note, in case the local sheriff drives by. I don't want you arrested for trespassing or for digging for treasure that isn't there." She laughed a second time in a thin, high-pitched voice. Franklin joined in her laughter, although he snorted more through his nose than laughed with his voice.

"Here you go," the woman said as she handed me the note. "One written note allowing you to inspect the property, dig holes, and look in the windows. Remember, don't leave any unfilled. There have been plenty of people with metal detectors, but they never found a thing. Have a good time. Bye."

Franklin called out, "Stay dry!" They waved us out of the office. Raul and I climbed into the station wagon. Granma pulled out of the parking lot and turned. We drove toward Chennault Plantation.

Chapter Nineteen

The drive took fifteen minutes. Granma pulled into the visitor's lot and turned off the engine. She turned to us and said, "Bettah get goin' while no one else is here."

Raul climbed out from the back seat. I opened my door and stepped on the wet cement driveway. We walked toward the house. "Be back inna hour. If not, I'll send Malcolm aftah y'all," Granma called after us. "Wait, I've got somethin' for yo'."

I turned and trudged back to the car. Raul stopped walking and waited for me half-way between the car and Chennault Manor. "Here, these are for yo'. They'll help yo' find the gold."

I stared at the metal thingies. "Wha' are they?"

"Divinin' rods. Used 'em when I was a chile. Yo' be…"

"Divinin' rods? Don' they help yo' find watah?"

"They find whatevah yo' wan' 'em t' find."

I clasped them tight, got out of the car, and rejoined Raul.

"Wha' are those?" he asked.

"Divinin' rods."

"Yo've got t' be kiddin'!"

"Granma swears by 'em."

Raul shrugged his shoulders. "I don' have her faith."

"Granma gave 'em t' me. She's drivin'. Wha' do we have t' loose?"

"If yo' want t' look stupid, tha's yar choice." Raul said. "She's yo' granma. Just don' stick my eyes out with 'em"

The vision I had of Chennault Plantation during my spirit journey had prepared me for its old southern splendor charm. It was a two-story house with six white columns supporting the second floor. Two large oak trees stood on either side of the house, their orange leaves framing the upper story.

We climbed up the brick steps, walked to one large double window and peeked in. The room was empty. I saw a double staircase winding up out of the room, and two fireplaces.

"Not much to see." Raul said.

"I don' feel good." I stopped talking. Raul and I stepped down the front stairs. I shivered. A shadow passed over me. I felt chilled to the bone, but that was impossible. It must have been because we were no longer sheltered by the house. Raul shifted from foot to foot. I shared his uneasiness. Several raindrops fell on my head. I shook it and looked up. The sky was full of racing black and gray clouds. "We should get back to the station wagon."

I never heard him or saw him.

"Are you listening to me?" Raul asked.

I was alone in a black void. The plantation house and Raul had disappeared. I had become a black Confederate soldier. My wagonmate urged me to take three sacks of gold and bury them. I stepped down from the wagon. The grass was wet. I trudged one hundred yards from the wagon, halfway to the house's porch. I squirmed under watchful eyes.

The day's coldness increased. Sweat coated my tee shirt.

A bush branch moved with the wind. I turned and stared. A whippoorwill called out to its mate. Something touched my bare arm. My blood ran cold. My heart stopped beating. Afraid, I whispered, "Raul?"

"I'm ovah here, Anna Mae," Raul's voice echoed. I jerked my head up. I looked back. Raul stood by the porch steps. He hadn't walked into the center of the yard as I had. Vibrations shook both my hands. I glanced at the rods. I had forgotten all about them.

"Walk around!" Raul shouted. "See where they take you!"

I trampled over the lawn. The rods pulled sideways they circled twice and split apart. I stopped walking when they pointed towards one spot on the ground.

I gasped. "Get a shovel!" I yelled and hopped from foot to foot. "Use yo' hands and start diggin'."

Raul plopped to his knees by the spot. He started digging with both hands. The time stretched on for what seemed like forever. A plastic coat sleeve struck me. I jumped and turned. Malcolm stood behind me, huddled in Granma's poncho. "Wha' do yo' want? Scared me half t' death!"

"Granma told me to give you this." Malcolm held out a shovel. "She packed it in the station wagon last night, and forgot to tell you. Here, you take it. It's heavy." Malcolm handed the shovel to me. He hurried back to the car, clutching Granma's poncho around him.

I threw the shovel toward Raul. He caught it. He placed the shovel's pointed end into the dirt, put his left boot on its edge, and pushed it into the dirt. He tossed up one shovel of dirt and kept digging. It went a lot faster with the shovel.

I really didn't believe we would find anything, including water. I was wrong. I heard a clink and a chink. The shovel had hit something solid.

"It's probably a large stone." Raul said. He held the shovel poised for the next thrust.

"It sounds solid. Dig deepah, and let's see. It might be somethin' othahh than a stone!"

Raul dug deeper and widened the hole. He stopped. I saw a piece of rope pushing through the dirt.

"It can't be!" I stooped and braced my hands on my knees so I could get a better look. Nothing was gonna get by me. I'd make sure of that.

Raul crouched, handing me the shovel. He poked his face closer into the hole.

"Try untyin' it."

He reached out and grabbed the rope with his hands. Raul unwound the rope from the neck of a sack.

I put the shovel on the dirt beside me. I bent over and stared into the opening. Something bulged inside the bag. I shook my head. "I don' believe this. Touch it. See if its solid or not."

Raul grasped the bag and felt it. He pushed one hand inwards. It clunked. Raul looked up. We exchanged glances. I couldn't believe our luck. Without thinking, I started gabbing. "Tha' realtor told us no one found any buried gold at Chennault Plantation for ovah a hundred years. How could they miss it when it's in plain sight?"

Stunned, Raul stumbled over his answer. "Not sure...less they didn't think the gold would be buried so close to the house."

"Bettah get Malcolm. We'll need him t' carry the gold to the car"

"There might be more bags. Should we try and find 'em?"

"Hmm. In my vision, one Negro soldier told his wagonmate t' bury several bags. Yo' win. Let's keep diggin'."

Raul paused. "Tell yo' wha'. Go and ask yo' Granma t' back up the car. We can lift one bag at a time into the station wagon's rear trunk door. Oh yeah, don' forget 'bout Malcolm. He'll nevah forgive us if he isn' part of this."

I grinned. "Yo' so right."

In the end, Raul ran back to the car. I saw Granma lower her window. Raul leaned in. Malcolm opened the side door and stepped out. I heard the engine start. Malcolm returned with Raul. Granma arrived two seconds later, with the wagon's trunk door facing us.

Raul picked up the shovel by the hole. He dug deeper and broadened the hole to three feet wide and about as deep. Raul and I weren't too surprised to see another tied rope sticking through the dirt. He dug around the sack and hit its side with the shovel. We heard another clink.

Around me, voices floated in and out of my hearing. I strained, standing on tip-toes to catch what was being said. At first I thought I heard Malcolm's voice, but I was wrong. More voices joined the lone voice. The voices kept getting louder, as if several people approached me from behind and were almost standing beside me. I tried locating them, but I saw no one except Granma, Raul, and Malcolm.

I pulled at Malcolm's arm. He glanced at me and put his arm around my waist, as if he sensed something was wrong. The warmth from him calmed me, but inside my stomach was still flip-flopping. I waited. The voices came closer. They shouted. I felt cold air flash across my face. A heavy mixture of tobacco and coffee crept up into my nostrils. I sucked in my breath and waited. My body rigid, I didn't dare move.

The voices passed in front of me. Five seconds later, I couldn't hear them at all. I shook my head. I looked at the ground and saw no footprints in the mud. I shivered. The rain dripped down my neck and my back. Malcolm pressed my arm and thrust his face into mine.

"Are you all right? You look like you've seen a ghost!"

Granma chose that second to appear. She joined Malcolm and stared down into the hole that Raul had dug.

Granma clasped her hands and did a pantomime of a person in pain. Her body twisted. Her arms twined. She cocked her head off to one side and said in a perilous voice, "Wha' will they say?" Her look was so comical that all of us burst into laughter.

I kept quiet about my encounter. Instead, I said, "Three sacks, I'm hopin' we can find two more."

"I'll keep diggin'. There's got to be two, or maybe even three more." Raul grinned.

"Did the rods work out all right?"

"I found the gold."

"I thought yo' might. I 'ways found wha' I wanted with 'em"

Raul kept digging. Two other bags appeared under the dirt. "We now have five bags. Tha's plenty."

"How come?"

"Are you kiddin'? Those soldiers didn' have all tha' much time t' bury the gold. The Union Army was breathin' down their necks. They didn' have time t' do anythin' 'cept bury a few bags. We're lucky we found them at all," Raul said.

Granma looked at Raul. "He's right. Confederate soldiers expectin' Union troops wouldn' take 'nough time t' bury more than three or four bags without gettin' caught. Are y'all ready t' go t' our next stop—Sandersville?"

Raul and I exchanged glances. "Let's load the car first."

Raul tapped his head. "Good thinking," He placed the shovel on the dirt edge around the hole. Malcolm reached down into the hole and tried lifting one bag. He dropped the bag.

"Too heavy," he gasped.

"Probably weighs as much as yo' do, if not more. I've backed up the car as close as I dare. Raul and Anna Mae, join hands. Put your hands under the bag. Malcolm,yo' hold the bag by its top. 'Tween the three of yo', the bags should make it int' the station wagon. I've opened the rear door."

"Thanks for packin' the shovel. Here, hold my rods, please?"

Granma smiled and hugged me. She reached out and took the rods. I spent the next thirty minutes helping Raul lift up all the gold bags. With Malcolm's help, we carried the four bags to the car. Raul and I placed them on the floor and pushed them inside. When all four bags were in, Raul grasped the metal handle on the rear door and slammed it shut.

Malcolm went back for the shovel. He dragged it on the dirt. When he reached the wagon, Raul picked it up and placed it on the car's floor. He and Malcolm climbed in. I walked to the other side, opened the door and slid into the seat. Granma turned her head. "Malcolm, go back and fill in tha' hole with dirt. We don' want anyone t' fall in."

Malcolm pushed himself out of the car. He trudged back to the hole, dragging the shovel behind him. Using its side, he pushed the dirt back in until the hole was filled. He tramped on top of the dirt and stomped it down until it was level with the rest of the ground. He plodded back, once again dragging the shovel. Raul opened the side door and took the shovel from Malcolm. Malcolm climbed in, closed the door, and sat back with his arms crossed against his shirt. "Okay, Granma?"

"Thank yo'. Yo' my big boy."

Malcolm smiled, all of his white teeth exposed. She gave me the rods, then put the key into the ignition. The motor started. She had turned the steering wheel to the right to get back onto pavement when I saw him in the side view mirror: Pit Bull's father!

"We've got company," I said.

Chapter Twenty

Mr. Paxton jumped out of his pickup truck and slammed its door. A Confederate license plate graced the front of his truck. I saw a three-tier gun rack with two rifles resting sideways inside, behind the rear seat. A link chain held them in place.

I gulped as Mr. Paxton swaggered to Granma's side of the station wagon.

"What are y'all doing here?"

Granma stiffened, but she didn't back down. "Good mornin'. Beautiful day, isn' it?"

Raul and I kept our faces straight and looked forwards. Malcolm picked up his copy of *Dare Detectives* and directed his concentration into the page. Raul whistled "Dixie" and I hummed along. Pit Bull's daddy scanned the inside of the station wagon. I held my breath. His eyes traveled down the length of the car, over the back seat and into the trunk area. I released my breath. He glared at Granma. "My boy don' lie. We all know who started that fire. Beats me why they haven' come and arrested the lot of y'all. I heard they're grounded until further notice."

"Haven' heard tha'. The kids are with me so y'all are safe."

Mr. Paxton snorted. He turned his head and spat tobacco juice on the ground. He laughed, in a false booming voice. I winced, but I kept quiet. Granma put the car into reverse. The car rolled back about an inch. Pit Bull's daddy released the window and stepped away.

Mr. Paxton scowled. He tried staring Granma down. Granma kept her eyes locked on him. I checked my wristwatch. Pit Bull's daddy noticed me. He pressed his thick lips together and then stuck out his hands and grabbed the window's ledge. "I'm not in the habit of issuing warnin's, but..."

"Then don' and yo' won' get hurt," Granma said, her voice louder than Pit Bull's daddy's.

"I don' think I made myself clear. 'Til yo' granddaughtah is cleared by the fire marshal and the police, I suggest she stays at home and outta trouble."

Granma licked her lips. "I don' have t' answer t' yo'. It's a fact tha' my young'un is workin' on a school project for history class. A friend is workin' with her. Even though school is closed, I 'spect tha' Ms. Yolanda would want 'em t' finish it...'less...yo'..got problems...with...that."

Mr. Paxton's face froze and turned redder than any barn door I'd ever seen. He lifted his fingers from the window's ledge, took three steps back from the wagon and glared. His cheeks puffed out and he breathed hard as he told us off. "I never come 'tween a teacher and a student. I'm keepin' both of my eyes on yo'. If yo' granddaughtah is seen without yo', she's in a heap a trouble. Do I make myself clear, ma'am?"

Granma gave him a Cheshire cat smile. "I hear yo'. My young'un won' be goin' out without me, and tha's tha'. One more thin', people-baitin' ain't allowed no more. It's 'gainst the law."

Pit Bull's daddy's face contorted. Granma and Mr. Paxton locked horns. He lost, fair and square. Mr. Paxton withdrew his eyes and let go of the car's window. He laughed crazy, like a hyena howling at the moon, and choked out his reply."Goodday t' yo', ma'am." He even lifted his cowboy hat from his sparse, thinning brown hair.

Pit Bull's daddy walked back to his pickup truck. He got in, started the engine, put the car in reverse and roared off.

Granma pulled on to the concrete pad, then turned to me. "Let's eat!"

After lunch Granma took the Georgia map from the seat. She pointed her finger at the route she'd outlined in marker to Sandersville. "We go southwest on Georgia 44. Then we come to Graball Road and take it toward Hoyt Lane, and continue, followin' Georgia 44. We turn left ont' Georgia 17 south—Sam McGill Memorial Parkway, north bypass east—then continue t' follow Georgia 17 south. We turn right ont' Georgia 80. Georgia 80 becomes East Cadley Road. We then turn right ont' Old Greensboro Road, and then a left ont' Church Street."

She glanced up from the map and scrutinized my face. I closed my eyes. The name didn't click. I opened them. "Sorry Granma, it's nothin'."

She shrugged and glanced down at the map. "We turn left ont' Atlanta Highway, which is US 278, then we take Georgia 12, which is the same as Jefferson Davis Memorial Highway. We continue t' follow Atlanta Highway. We then turn right ont' Georgia 16—the Macon Highway. We turn left ont' Georgia 123, which is the same as Shoals Road. We continue t' follow Shoals Road until we turn left ont' Hamburg State Park Road, which is also Georgia 248."

Again, Granma stopped reading the map, paused and looked up at me. I looked back at her, my eyes squinting. "Macon sounds familiar. I'm sure there was a Macon when Davis was on the run."

"Nothin' else?" Granma asked.

I shook my head. "Nope, nothin'"

She returned her attention back to the map. "On Georgia 248 we turn slightly t' the right ont' Georgia 102, which is also called Mitchell Road. We follow Georgia 102, or Mitchell Road, till it becomes Georgia 15. On East Church Street we take a left. And we're there, in Sandersville, Georgia, USA."

"Do we pass the town of Warthen?"

Granma studied the map. "Yeah, why?"

"Tha' town sounds familiar. My history textbook mentions tha' the wagon train passed through Warthen and then continued south t' Sandersville. He arrived there in the afternoon on May sixth. Davis left Sandersville and traveled toward the Oconee River, near Ball's Ferry. He'd hoped t' camp there for the night.

"At Irvington, Davis was approached by a Confederate spy who warned him 'bout Federal troops bein' half a day's journey from him and the wagon train."

"Now I understand," Raul said from the back seat. "Davis did plan on returning the gold to France, but he didn't succeed. The wagon train carrying the gold got as far as Chennault, then it was stolen or ambushed."

Granma pushed her face into mine. "Yo' 'kay, Anna Mae? Y'r eyes rolled back and the whites showed. Yo' head fell forward on yo' chest."

"I'm fine. When do the Garcias join us?" I asked, changing the subject, hoping that Granma would leave it alone. She studied my face.

"I tole yo' 'fore. They waitin' for us on Georgia 44. It turns int' Graball Road and continues toward Hoyt Lane."

"Didja say Warthen Road?" My stomach rolled. My vision blurred. I punched the automatic window button hard. The window slid down. I lifted my body and hung my neck out over the window. Gagging and coughing, up came lunch, or what was left of it. I wiped my mouth with the back of my hand. My entire body felt limp and cold.

"Yo' okay?" Malcolm piped up from the rear seat.

"Somethin' I ate." I shrugged my shoulders, but Granma wasn't fooled.

"Yo' sight spoke true and tha's scarin' yo' t' death." She glanced back at the map. "It should take two hours, longah if we stop at Warthen, and y'all do some diggin'." Granma placed the map in her lap and gripped the steering wheel. She put the car in reverse, eased off the pad and drove out to the street. We passed a white Cadillac on Graball Road. It was the Garcia's. Abuelita waved as we drove past them. They followed behind the station wagon, keeping a 10-foot space between us.

The day remained dark and dull. I stared out the window, looking at wet grass, dripping tree branches, and puddles that lay in the road. Not many cars passed us in either direction. The road belonged to Granma and Raul's grandparents.

My eyes closed, lulled by the sameness of the day and countryside. I sat upright. An electric bolt pulsed through me, running up my legs, arms and chest until it crested at my scalp. My short hairs stood at attention.

I was no longer sitting in a car traveling forty-five miles an hour. I was inside a city house, running up a winding staircase. In my hand, I held a piece of paper. I shouted as I ran. "He came through! I've got it."

My wife met me at the top of the stairs. She raised her hands and covered both ears. "Stop shouting, Mumford, and tell me! Who came through?"

"He divided it amongst us. He says, 'Do with it as you see fit.' Do you not see? We can use this for children orphaned by the war and restore our beloved plantation."

My other self faded. I touched the seat. The cloth knotted beneath my hand. I was back in the station wagon, traveling toward Sandersville. I felt weak and confused. I picked up my water bottle and gulped it down. The water brought me more into the present. I finished drinking and stowed the bottle in the cup holder.

I saw Raul's eyes reflected in the rear view mirror. His eyes stared into mine, as did Malcolm's.

"Wha's happenin'?" Malcolm asked.

"Just thinkin'."

"Any nudges?" Granma asked.

"Nope."

"Yo' let me know when yo' do. Should be happenin' soon,"

"All right." I dropped my eyes and stared out the window. How dull. I yawned, then stretched my arms above my head. They hit the car's ceiling. My bones cracked. I stiffened. A chill crept down my spine.

Another hour passed. Granma pulled to the right side of the road. "I need a nap. Why don' y'all get out of the car and walk 'round a bit? Gimme 10 minutes and I'll be good to go."

"Pile out, guys." In the rear view mirror, the Garcia's pulled up behind us and stopped. They remained in their car.

Raul opened the wagon's side door. He clambered out, followed by Malcolm. I opened the front door and stepped out. The door closed by itself. I shivered. The chill hadn't left me. It deepened. I walked around the front end of the car and onto the dirt and pebbled grass. Raul and Malcolm joined me. Tall weeds, beer cans and wet picnic tables dotted the vacant lot.

"Spooky," Malcolm said as he pumped his arms up and jumped, with his feet wide apart.

I looked at him. "In wha' way?"

"Bored is more like it." Raul chimed in.

"Can' be too long," I said.

"Any hunches?" Raul asked with a grin.

"Not a nibble!"

"Darn! I hoped yo'd find some more. I wanted t' surprise Momma and Poppa," Malcolm said.

"Yo' finished?"

Malcolm stopped jumping like a Mexican jumping bean. We headed back toward the car. Raul and Malcolm opened the rear door. They climbed in. I continued walking to the front of the car. The door opened. I felt chilled again. This spooked me, but I said nothing. As I slid into the car I struck my head with the flat of my palm. I turned and focused on Raul. "How many bags of gold make up $600,000?"

"It depends how many gold bars were put into each bag. It also depends on the weight of each bar inside that bag. How much was the value of an ounce of gold in 1861?"

Raul cocked his head. He mumbled numbers under his breath. Three minutes passed. Raul locked eyes with me. "About 28."

"If yo' had t' bury 28 sacks, how would yo' get 'em past marchin' soldiers, pryin' eyes, or the enemy?"

"Hide 'em, silly."

"Where?"

Malcolm yelled out the answer before Raul collected his breath. "False bottoms! That's what that clue meant. Those wagons had false bottoms built under them. They stored the gold that way."

Raul's eyes glittered. In a thoughtful voice, he added, "The wagons stopped for the night at Sandersville."

I could see both Malcolm's and Raul's breaths in the mirror. They frosted, as each breathed in and out. I breathed into my hand. The vapor cooled my palm. I glanced at Granma. Her opened window kept her side of the car cool, not cold. Like a slap in the face, I yipped. "Those wagons would pass three small towns 'long the way:

Warthen, Warrenton, and Washington."

"Let's not forget that Jefferson Davis gave some of the gold to his cabinet while the rest traveled south. In my spirit journey, I remember Mary Anne's father telling his daughter he buried 30 loose coins between Sandersville and Chennault Plantation. It makes sense that he would've buried them in marked spots that he could find again." The chill didn't go away; I shivered in spite of the heat.

Numbers slid by in my mind as I counted them backwards, starting from 100. My toes numbed out, followed by my calves and legs. I placed my hands in my lap and allowed them to go limp. I traveled inwards to a place where I felt comfortable and safe.

My mind whirled as I ticked off the facts and made myself remember them. Mary Ann's father was the Methodist minister. The Pinkerton Agency arrested the entire Chennault family and brought them in for questioning in Washington, D. C. Police and military guardsmen roamed the streets. Security was tight. Pinkerton's took no chances with any of us. They sequestered us in separate rooms. An endless drill of questions proceeded and kerosene lamps were lit and thrust into our faces. Shouting! Threats! Hollering! Hot! I can't breathe!

They're shouting at me, asking again and again, "Where's the gold?" I didn't know. Papa didn't tell me where. All he said was that he buried the coins where they couldn't find them.

Papa mentioned Warthen. You won't tell Papa. He would be angry that a true Southern woman couldn't keep a secret.

I twisted on the seat. My head fell forward with a jerk. I opened my eyes. The car spun. The dashboard loomed in front of my eyes. A thick stump reached for my chin. I ducked.

"Chile, yo' is safe." Granma smiled. She stroked the side of my cheek. In a soft voice, she said, "We passed Warthen thirty minutes ago. We'll drive back. When we get there, I'll drive real slow. Iff'n yo' feel somethin', holler. I'll stop the car. Take the divinin' rods with yo'. I'll wait right here in the car." She patted the seat, then pushed in the hazard lights switch on the dash board.

They lit up green, and blinked. The Garcias pulled around us and made a U-turn fifteen feet up the road. Granma backed the wagon up and turned back toward Warthen. In the rearview mirror I saw the Cadillac following us.

As we approached Warthen, I emptied my mind a second time. No visions. Granma drove at 15 miles an hour. Raul and Malcolm sat on the edge of the back seat. Malcolm put *Dare Detectives* face down on the seat. Granma drove through Warthen. When we got to the outskirts, I felt a dull ache twanging inside my head.

"Stop the car!" I yelled.

Granma stopped. Pale sunlight bathed the car, although a few cirrus clouds streaked the sky. The twanging gave way to an insistent pounding. I plucked the divining rods from the seat. They twisted and turned in my hands. I kicked open the door and stepped on the gravel road. The rods lurched and pulled me forward. *Not much to see, an abandoned field, lined with a white picket fence, broken in the middle.*

The back door creaked opened. The boys got out They joined me on the side of the road. "Yo' goin' north?" Raul asked.

I kept walking north. The rods tugged. I stepped over rotting, wooden boards. Raul and Malcolm flanked me on each side. The rods pulled me into waist-deep grass and weeds. I saw cows and bulls grazing in the distance.

The rods bounced and gave a final spin. Their ends pointed down. I stopped walking. Raul took one look at them and ran to the station wagon to get the shovel. Malcolm remained with me. Raul hurried back, carrying the shovel. He pushed its tip into the dirt and dug. On his first try, he came up with stones and pebbles mixed in with the soil. He threw the dirt off to one side.

Malcolm and I stepped away. Raul pushed the shovel into the dirt. The banks of the hole soon held a pile of dirt, chopped tree roots, stones, and rocks. The rods kept pointing down into the hole. I watched as Raul kept digging. Overhead, a plane's engine droned. The sun's heat engulfed us. The clouds disappeared. Sweat dripped down inside my slicker. I took it off and tied its sleeves around my waist. It blanketed the back of my legs.

Every now and then we would hear a false "clank." Raul stopped digging. I jumped into the hole. Crouching, I sifted the dirt through my fingers. Nothing! I stepped out of the hole with Malcolm's help, and Raul started digging once again. Malcolm helped Raul by rolling the larger rocks out of the way.

The hole became deeper, while its sides became larger. Raul didn't look up. He stopped once, spat on his hands, and then grasped the shovel handle again. Malcolm stood by me. It started to rain again. He clutched Granma's poncho and pulled it around his thin body.

Raul stopped digging. He crouched.

"Hold the shovel, will ya?" he said as he handed the shovel to me. Raul, with Malcolm's help, dragged a large rock from the center of the hole. I stared down into it. A piece of rope stuck out.

"There's somethin' down there. Keep diggin'," I ordered. My body tingled. Blood rushed up to my face. I wanted to sing and dance, but I didn't. First, I handed the shovel back to Raul, and then I folded my arms across my chest and just waited.

Malcolm got out of Raul's way and watched, knowing that he couldn't lift the big stones by himself anymore. Raul proceeded to dig. We soon saw several more bags.

"Think there's more?"

"Only way t' find out is t' keep diggin'." I wanted to scream, "Yes!"

Raul dug for another fifteen minutes. He widened the hole and dumped the extra dirt off to the other side of the hole. That pile of dirt grew higher and higher. Malcolm crossed his legs.

"I've gotta go," he whined.

"Yo' jokin', right?" Raul asked in between spurts of breath.

"Not 'gain. Go undah a bush far 'way so we can' see yo'. Here!" I whipped out a crumbled tissue from my pocket. "Take it and git!"

Raul smiled. "Trust yo' brothahh t' have t' go now." In his next breath, Raul added, "Geronimo!"

I looked down. He was right. More tied burlap bags lay in the hole. "How much gold do yo' think there is?"

He started counting. "One, two, three, four...ten...bags in all."

"Holy cow!"

Raul stared up at me. "We know that some of it was found by the Yankees and the rest. We'll nevah know who found it. One of us should ask yo' Granma t' back up the wagon so we can load it from here."

Raul stuck the shovel in the dirt. It stood upright like a beacon in the rain for Granma to see.

"I'll go." I turned and looked at the car. I sucked in my breath. Two black Confederate soldiers glared at me. Their hands were empty.

Chapter Twenty-one

"Anna Mae, what's up?"

Raul pushed his face into mine. I hadn't heard him climb out of the hole or walk towards me.

"Those soldiers..." I pointed at the car. Raul squinted. He shielded his eyes with his right hand. "Nope, just two cars—yo' station wagon and Abuelito's Cadillac. Can' see anyone standin' out in the rain 'cept us."

I squirmed.

"They're there, standin' next t' the car, their arms outstretched, palms up." I closed my eyes, then reopened them. The black soldiers still stood in front of me, with muddied faces, torn trousers, faded jackets and cracked boots. Their bare toes wiggled through their shoes' tears. I turned back towards the hole with a sudden thought: *Where's Malcolm?*

Raul twisted his head. "Bathroom break, here he comes!"

Malcolm ran back toward us. A sudden wind caught Granma's poncho. It blew up and attacked him. Both of his hands sailed up. He flattened it as he rejoined us. "Feel bettah?" I asked.

"Yeah," he said as he wiped his hands on his jeans. *Ugh! Boys!* I thought and pushed down a gag. Malcolm raised his eyes to Raul.

"Nothin' happened. We were waitin' for yo'."

"Is it my turn t' get Granma and yo' grandparents?" Malcolm asked.

"Bettah yo' than me," I said.

"Nothin' doin'. I'll go and get yo' granma, then I'll tell Abuelito and Abuelita what's up. Yo' two stay put," Raul ordered us. I glanced at Malcolm. We exchanged secret grins. We waited until Raul turned his back and walked to the car. I hopped into the ditch first, then Malcolm jumped in. We crouched and eyed the tied burlap bags. Malcolm poked at one of them with his forefinger. "How much do yo' reckon?"

I counted his ten fingers. "Tha' many," I said.

"Oh boy!" Malcolm rubbed his hands together.

"We'd bettah get outta here 'fore Mr. High and Mighty returns." I added under my breath. Malcolm must've heard me. He clambered out of the hole. He stretched his left hand out. I grabbed it. He dragged me up out of the hole. Out of breath, our hearts pounding, we waited for Raul, Granma, and the Garcias to join us.

We didn't have long to wait. I spotted the station wagon as it drove toward us. Raul wasn't in the front seat. It was Abuelito instead. I looked at Malcolm. His eyes were fixed on something else. I shivered. The station wagon backed up and stopped about five feet away from us.

Abuelito opened his door and stepped out first. Granma's door opened too, as if she decided to join us outside. I heard two doors slam shut. Their noise ricocheted. I didn't see Raul at all.

"Hi, Abuelito," Malcolm said.

Abuelito grinned. "A long trip, but worth it, from what Raul says. He stayed behind in the Caddy with Abuelita to explain things."

"Did Raul tell yo' everythin'?

Abuelito's eyes sparkled. "Certainly."

"Can yo' help us carry the bags and load them int' the car?"

"That's what I'm here for," Abuelito said.

He strode past me and looked down into the ditch. He counted out loud. "*Uno, dos, tress, cuatro, cinco, seis, siete, ocho, nueve, diez*. That's quite a haul. Hmm, I might need Raul's help after all. I'll be right back."

Abuelito climbed out of the gully and walked toward his Cadillac. He returned with Raul. "Swing open the wagon's rear door. Spread out the blankets that Zora placed there this morning. When you're finished, join me, Anna Mae, and Malcolm by the hole. I've got an idea."

We waited for Raul as he completed Abuelito's request. Raul swung the wagon's rear door opened. I saw him spread three blankets out on the floor, each end meeting the other's end. Raul trotted back. His grandfather gathered us into a small circle. He placed his arms around Raul's shoulders. Raul placed his arms around Malcolm's shoulders. Malcolm placed his arms around my shoulders.

"Now that the circle is complete, here's what we're going to do. Raul, you and Anna Mae will lift the burlap bag together out of the hole. Hand it to me. I'll place it on the ground. Malcolm will steady me as I climb out of the hole, then I'll pick up the bag. You and Anna Mae will weave your hands together and place them under the bag for support. Malcolm, you go first and make sure the ground is smooth so none of us stumble."

When we got to the car, Malcolm climbed into the rear. "One, two, three!" I said. We hoisted the bulging bag and placed it on the floor. Malcolm pulled while Raul pushed it from behind.

"Everyone clear?" Abuelito asked.

I nodded "yes." Malcolm grinned from ear to ear. Abuelito beamed. Raul and I exchanged sly looks. For the moment, peace and happiness reigned. With our fingers laced, Raul and I bent down, hefting the first bag of gold from underneath. Abuelito grabbed the bag from us. He dumped it on the dirt beside the hole. With Malcolm's help, Abuelito stepped out of the hole and picked up the bag. Raul and I followed behind. We climbed out of the hole and again wove our fingers together. Together the three of us plodded to the station wagon while Malcolm scampered ahead and kicked some large stones out of our way.

When we arrived at the car, Abuelito, Raul and I lifted the bag and set it inside. Raul pushed from behind. Malcolm pulled it towards him. The total operation took forty-five minutes. When the last bag was pulled and pushed in, Malcolm jumped out.

"Watch your fingers! Abuelito yelled as he slammed the rear door shut.

"We bettah fill tha' hole. We don' want t' leave evidence. Oh, and the shovel—I 'most forgot it," I said to Raul.

He trotted back to the freshly dug soil. Raul scooped the dirt back into the hole with the side of the shovel. It took him five minutes. When he was finished, Raul jumped on top of the dirt and stomped it down. He marched back and forth until the dirt blended in with the surrounding pebbled and rock infested grass.

I watched from beside the car. Malcolm had crawled into the back seat too, complaining about his tired feet and aching back. Granma's voice droned in the background, talking to Abuelito about something, but my eyes and heart were focused on Raul. Even caked with mud and dirt, I loved looking at him.

Raul soon joined me, dragging the shovel behind him. He stooped, as if too tired to see that I was waiting for him. At the last minute, Raul dropped the shovel on the matted grass and went around to the front passenger seat. He opened the door and bowed, with a cockeyed grin.

"Madame," Raul said. He swung his arm before him like a 16th century knight. Granma's eyes warmed my back. I shrugged and smiled.

"Thanks, kind sir." I fled into the front seat.

Raul slammed the door shut.

He walked back around to the front of the car and waved. My eyes followed him. Raul stooped and lifted the shovel so its handle rested on his shoulder. Raul opened the side door and threw the shovel onto the carpeted car floor. I heard it clang against the seat. He slid in and closed the door.

Abuelito sauntered to his Cadillac. I saw Abuelita stretch across the seat and tug at the car handle until the door opened. He stepped in, doubling over. I watched the Cadillac. It rocked back and forth as if the ground was shakings. The station wagon didn't budge. That bothered me. I couldn't place my finger on why. I scrunched my eyes and waited for whatever it was to surface. Nothing!

"Buckle yo' seatbelt," Malcolm reminded everyone.

Granma buckled hers and made sure I buckled mine. "Where t' next?"

"We need a safe place t' stow the loot. Got any bright ideas?" I spoke to the rear view mirror. Raul and Malcolm's eyes blinked in unison.

"Bury it," Malcolm said first.

I scowled. "I don' think so."

"That's what pirates do aftah they steal someone's gold. They bury it."

"We could take it to the bank," Raul suggested.

Granma laughed so hard that she had to hold her sides. Her eyes teared up. I didn't see anything funny about it. "Wha's the joke?"

Granma coughed. She wiped her eyes with the back of her hand. "Y'all are not thinkin'. How are yo' gonna 'splain t' the bank where yo' got all tha' money. I don' think they will take yo' word tha' yo' found it buried in the ground."

I groaned. "She's right. Hadn' thought 'bout tha'. Wha' will they think at the bank?"

"'Prob'ly think we stole it," Raul said. "I mean wha' with the fire and all."

"Tha's right. Rub it in. I didn' see yo' git 'cused of startin' the darn thin'."

"If tha's the way yo' feel 'bout it, Mrs. Kingsley, stop the car. I'll git out now. I don' have t' take this sittin' down."

"Stop it, both of y'all. If yo' don' stick togethah yo' will fall 'part." Granma said.

"I've heard tha' 'fore. Now where?" I asked.

"Yo' not the only one who reads, chile. I'll ask Miguel. He must know someone who can help us out. The Garcias have lived here since the 1600s. 'Nough time t' get t' know a few folk. We're t' meet Raul's grandparents at yo' poppa's and momma's house."

I had nothing to say after that. My brain froze; the words seemed like they were dead on my tongue, buried in my mouth. Granma started the engine. It wheezed, pinged, coughed and died. The rain picked up. Large drops splattered and pelted the car's roof, hammering the metal so hard that it reminded me of rattling drums and marching feet.

Granma twisted the car key a second time. This time the engine caught. She put the car in "drive." We pulled out onto the main road. Abuelito followed in their Cadillac.

I rested my head back against the cushioned headrest and watched the rain streak the front windshield, and then trickle into the windshield wiper's arched path. Swaying trees, over-filled drains, and huddled cows seemed to zip by me as we drove along at 45 miles per hour.

Too tired to think, my head nodded. I couldn't keep my eyelids open any longer. The toothpick trick sounded like a great idea to prop my lids opened. Too bad, we didn't have any. The last noise I heard was the tires smacking the road and squealing on the soaked asphalt.

Chapter Twenty-two

The Garcias followed us home. Granma pulled into the driveway first. She clicked on the garage door opener and the door lifted. Granma drove the wagon in, but didn't close the garage. I got out of the station wagon first, taking my backpack and divining rods with me. Raul and Malcolm exited the car to each side. Granma got out and walked to the side door of the garage that led into the house. She inserted the key into the lock and opened it.

Lavender and cinnamon struck my nostrils first. I inhaled, then shivered. The phone rang. I rushed inside to pick it up. The ringing kept banging inside my brain like a warning. I picked up the phone. Dead air greeted me.

"Hello? This is Anna Mae Botts. Can I help you? Hello? Hello?"

Granma joined me. She took the phone.

"Hello? Hello? This is Zora Kingsley. May I help yo?" She held the phone out between us. We both listened and heard—nothing. Granma placed the phone back in the cradle.

"They'll call back if it's important. Go and get outta yo' wet clothes'."

Raul and Malcolm traipsed into the kitchen. They left muddy sneaker prints on the floor. Granma frowned. Malcolm and Raul removed their sneakers. I eyed the mess, but I didn't volunteer to clean it up.

"Get the mop and clean it up." Granma snapped.

I kicked off my sneakers and threw them down on the doormat in front of the back door. Malcolm and Raul held onto theirs and eventually copied what I had done. Malcolm trudged to the utility closet and took out the mop. He set it on the floor and swiped at the muddy footprints. Granma breathed hard through her nostrils like a dragon. I waited for some fire to follow.

"Tha's not how yo' wash a floor. Give me tha' and watch. I ain't gonna do this 'gain." She grasped the mop handle with both hands. Granma took the mop to the sink and ran hot water from the faucet. She rinsed it and then wrung the cloth threads.

Smacking the mop on the floor, Granma wiped up all the prints. She took the mop back to the sink and rinsed it a second time. Malcolm walked up to the sink. Granma turned and handed him the mop.

"In the closet and make sure it's upside down," she snapped.

Malcolm gulped. I shrugged. Raul pantomimed. He held both fists up in front of his face, his right thumb signaling down. He placed his left hand on his hair and pointed to the top of the mop. Malcolm nodded and grinned. He carried the mop to the closet and set it right side up, with the cloth threads on top and the pole handle resting on the linoleum.

Granma walked to the table and sat down. "Figuah out where y'all want t' put tha' gold?"

I crossed my arms over my chest. I spread my legs far apart. My eyes narrowed. I snarled, "Not at the bank. I don' want it in the bank,"

"Abuelito and Abuelita should be here by now. I'll go get them and see what they have to say. Three extra heads are better than one," Raul said as he shot out of the room. He roared through the back door. It slammed shut. Granma and I locked eyes. Malcolm went to the refrigerator. I saw the light go on with my side vision. *Doesn't he ever think about anything except food and the bathroom?* I wondered.

The rear door squeaked as it opened. Raul walked in. His grandparents strode in behind him. His grandfather pulled out a chair for Abuelita. She sat down next to Granma. Her hands fluttered. She cleared her throat. Abuelita glanced at me, then at Raul, and then at Malcolm. She turned her eyes toward Granma.

"Zora, are you going to call the police?"

I shifted uneasily from one foot to the other. Raul and I exchanged glances. Malcolm plopped down on the floor. He held one of his books. Opening it, Malcolm started reading and kept his eyes glued to the page, lost to us.

Abuelito stood behind the chair Abuelita sat on. He grasped both of her shoulders and rubbed them. His gaze roamed the kitchen, and then settled on me.

"I think you should contact a lawyer, Zora, and get this mess straightened out. It's true the kids found the treasure, but they found it on private property and on the outskirts of Warthen Township. These kids need protection. Besides, that buried gold complicates things tremendously."

"Wha' 'bout all those newspaper's stories? The kids who find money in the streets. Don' they get a reward for turnin' it in? And, if the money isn' claimed in 30 days, the kids get to keep it?"

Malcolm muttered behind *Dare Detectives.* "Finders keepers, losers weepers."

"I don' know, chile. I read a story in the paper some time ago. The findah doesn' always get t' keep any of the monah, no mattah how long it takes. The police keep it for 'emselves." Granma said.

"Is that legal?" Raul asked.

Abuelito sucked in his cheeks. "I read that same article. The police cut a deal with the District Attorney. They kep' the money for themselves."

"Legal or not, that's what the article said. Some police departments keep found money. That's why, Zora, I suggest you contact a lawyer. If you don't know one, I have a good friend who's one. She'll be happy to help you and the children. Finding Jefferson Davis' lost Confederate money is a big deal. The South is still fightin' the War Between the States. We all know that. The fact that it was two African-American children and a Latino who found it will certainly stir up the locals, if not the federal government."

"There are the tax laws to consider, too." Abuelita said. "Since Anna Mae and Malcolm are under eighteen, their parents are responsible for paying those taxes."

"And so are we," Abuelito said.

The conversation took a wrong turn. I didn't like the way the adults took over.

"Can' we jus' get the gold outta the station wagon and hide it? 'Sides, I'm soaked to the bone. I wanna get outta these wet clothin'."

"Good idea, chile. Git t' the shed and git outta yo' wet clothin'. Raul, Malcolm, git goin' and change upstairs in Malcolm's room. Miguel, Juanita and I have some thinkin' t' do," Granma said, "When y'all saw tha' real estate person, did they give their okay for yo' t' walk and dig on Chennault?"

"Hold on. I forgot all 'bout somethin'." I dug the scrap of paper with the note on it out of my pants pocket. Pit Bull's daddy's unexpected visit had wiped my mind clean. "It's a bit damp. The ink ran. It's muddied, but yo'can still see the lady's name and date on it."

"Let me see it," Granma said.

I gave it to her, then I walked out to the shed. Raul and Malcolm had already left for upstairs. The last thing I heard was Granma's voice reading the note out loud. "The Lincoln County Development Authority gives Raul Garcia and Anna Mae Botts permission to visit Chennault Plantation and look for buried treasure. *If* and *when* they find such treasure—Jefferson Davis' lost Confederate gold—they have the Authority's permission to dig for it as long as they fill in the holes before they leave. Any gold they find belongs to them. Since there's no gold to be found, the Authority gives them permission. Signed, Charlotte Brown, September 7, 1994."

I reached the shed and walked into the room where I slid out of my wet Capris, shirt, underwear and socks. I threw the wet clothing into the hamper. Running the water, I rubbed myself with a washcloth and then toweled myself dry.

I pulled out my blue and gold sweat pants and a red tee shirt. I slipped my feet into the flip-flops and skipped back into the kitchen,

"Did I miss anythin'?" I asked.

Granma looked up. "It's a good thin' tha' there lady Charlotte Brown signed this lettah or y'all'd be in a heap of trouble."

"You're very lucky, you and Raul. It could be much worse," Abuelita said.

"We were told by the lady realtor tha' for the past 140 years folk have been diggin' on tha' plantation and nothin' was evah found. She and her friend had a good laugh on us. 'Sides, we told her it was a school project. The lady gave us the note right aftah we told her wha' it was for."

Malcolm and Raul entered the kitchen. Malcolm wore torn jeans and a bright orange shirt. Raul had borrowed one of Poppa's black sweatshirts and pants. He wore Poppa's slippers as well.

"I counted all tha' gold. We're loaded!" Malcolm shrieked.

"No, the money doesn' belon' t' us," Granma said. "Miguel, where can we put the gold 'till we get this mess straightened out?"

"Yo' givin' the gold t' the police? Yo' just said yo' didn' trust 'em!" I shouted at them.

"We're not givin' the gold t' just anyone. Miguel knows someone who can hep us." Granma said.

Abuelito stared at his wife. Abuelita rose from her chair. Abuelito stumbled backwards. She turned and threw herself at him. Abuelita twined her arms around Mr. Garcia's neck. She wept into his shirt. "No, Miguel! You promised me. No more."

Abuelito spoke over Abuelita's burst of words. "I have a friend who can help us. I've known him since Vietnam. If you all will excuse me, I saw a phone in your poppa's study."

Mr. Garcia removed his wife's arms from around his neck. She pushed him away, then sat down. Granma inched her chair closer to Abuelita and threw her arms around her. Abuelita leaned forward and pressed her head against Granma's chest.

Just like a soap opera, I thought. *How romantic*! Abuelito shoved the swinging doors on his way out of the kitchen. They bounced against the outside hallway. I heard his feet smack against the tiles. He headed towards Poppa's study. I heard the hinges of the study door open and the clunk of it shutting tightly.

"Anyone want somethin' to eat?" Granma asked. Both Raul and Malcolm nodded yes. *That figures. Malcolm's always hungry. Guess I am too,* I thought.

Granma went to the pantry and returned with three cans of vegetable chili. She opened them and emptied the contents into a saucepan. I headed to the refrigerator and took out a package of beef franks. Taking the scissors, I cut the plastic wrap and dumped the hot dogs into a plastic plate. Taking a sharp knife, I slit three openings in the dogs so they wouldn't burst. The microwave door swung opened. I watched it. My stomach flipped. No one else seemed to notice. I took the plate and placed it on the glass surface. The door closed when I removed my hands. A sudden coldness chilled my fingers.

I saw the timing pad push in all by itself. That did it! I backed off. Raul caught me.

"You okay? You're acting kind of strange."

I pointed at the microwave. The glass surface spun in a circle. The franks split and browned. Raul shrugged. I kept my eyes glued on the microwave. When the timer beeped, I reached forward. The door latch clicked, and the door swung open.

"Holy torpedoes!" Raul muttered into my left ear.

"Told yo'!"

I removed the franks and set them on the table. A spoon clattered on top of the range. I looked up. Granma stood in front of the oven and stirred the chili with her wooden spoon. She handed me the utensil, and walked to the table. Granma picked up the paring knife and cut the franks into one-inch pieces. I held out the pot of chili toward her. She pointed to the table. I placed the pot on a hot plate.

Granma took the cut-up franks and added them to the chili. "Set the table, Anna Mae. Raul, Malcolm, bring in some 'xtra chairs from the livin' room."

They left the kitchen without arguing. I retrieved the plates, glasses, and silverware. Abuelita twisted her Ankh in her hands. A soft light glowed from within it. I squinted and stared. Soft laughter erupted around me like a halo framing an angel's face. I glanced up. Nothing! Frustrated, I watched Granma as she finished putting supper together.

First she walked to the refrigerator and removed the vegetable bin from the bottom shelf. She took out a small head of lettuce, two green peppers, and one yellow onion. It shed some brown skin on the floor. I stooped and picked them up. She closed the refrigerator with her right foot. "Take out yo' poppa's wine."

I did as she requested. I took out Poppa's special holiday wine and placed the bottle on the table.

"Anne Mae, get the cheddah from the fridge."

When I returned with the cheese, Granma had placed three wine glasses on the table. In one of the wine glasses she poured half a glass of wine. She handed it to Abuelita.

"Thanks," she said and then took two quick sips, swallowed, and set the glass back on the table.

Raul and Malcolm chose that moment to step in from the dining room, carrying two chairs apiece. Malcolm struggled, balancing his in both hands. Raul held each chair easily.

Granma tossed the chopped green pepper, cheese and onion chunks into the chili. She tore sections of the lettuce leaves apart and arranged them on the plates. "Well, don' just stand there! Get the chairs up t' the table so we can all sit down."

Malcolm, Raul and I were given false wine to drink, known as grape juice. Abuelita served the chili to us. Abuelito still hadn't returned from his phone call. I put my napkin in my lap. Malcolm scrunched his up into a ball. I didn't notice what Raul did with his. I itched to know what Abueltio was saying to his friend.

After twenty minutes, Abuelito finally walked into the kitchen. Abuelita patted the chair beside her. "Sit down, Miguel. You're holding up supper."

Abuelito sat down. Granma ladled the chili onto his plate. Abuelita served him wine and poured a half glass for Granma.

"Is it settled?"

He smiled. "My friend, Armando, will be here in one hour. He will come in a borrowed Brinks armored car."

I stopped eating and flung my napkin on the table. "I don' like this."

Granma looked up. "Sit down, chile. Let's hear wha' Miguel has t' say 'fore we get mad."

I scowled. Abuelito ate a forkful of chili and chewed. He swallowed three sips of wine and put his glass down.

"Anna Mae, I'm not trying to cheat you, Malcolm or Raul. I'm surprised that you found anything at all. Most of the adults who've gone out searching for that gold have never found it. I'm proud of the way you three reasoned it out. My hat's off to you all."

"Let's face facts. You are under the age of 18. Your parents are out of town. Zora is your legal guardian until your parents return. Zora wants security for the gold. I have found one. Armando understands the situation. He's a field agent—a military intelligence officer. I'd trust him with my life."

I stared at Abuelito. "If yo' say so." I didn't want to give up. This was my first case. I had worked hard with Raul and Malcolm to solve it. I didn't feel like sharing it with anyone. I couldn't help it. We could use the money. I hated being poor and wearing cast offs and hand-me-down clothing. I knew that Abuelito could use some extra cash too. Raul wore clothes that were too big for him.

The cuffs on his pants were too wide. His coat sleeves hung over his hands. Even Granma needed a share of the money. I didn't want to give in like that. I wanted to fight, put up my dukes, as the cowboy always did in his movies.

Granma stared at me like she saw me for what I was, and not what she wanted me to be. She sighed. "You mustn' lose yo' faith, chile. It don't become yo'."

I picked up my glass of grape juice and gulped it down. I pretended that the juice was wine. Giddy, I felt suddenly macho. In a hardened voice, I said, "Let me get this straight. Yo' friend Armando takes the gold back with him and keeps it safe 'till Poppa and Momma gets back."

"That sums it up. You won't regret it. None of you will," Abuelito said.

I finished eating my chili. Once Raul, Malcolm, and I finished our chili, we were excused from the table and we left the kitchen. We went into the living room and watched television until Armando showed up.

Secret Agent Man Armando arrived at 7:30. The front doorbell sang out its usual song—Taps, Poppa's favorite melody. I got to my feet first and hurried toward the front door. Abuelito beat me to it. He opened the door and greeted Mr. Armando. He was a small, compact man. Everything he wore was black: his shirt, pants, and cowboy boots. He had a black walrus-like mustache that tucked into the corners of his mouth. His eyebrows grew together in one thick line across his forehead.

Abuelito showed him in and closed the door. Granma met them in the hallway. She escorted Mr. Armando into the living room. He chose Poppa's wing chair. It faced the door. His back was to the wall. Mr. Armando tipped the chair backward. He clasped his hands together, settled them in his lap and engulfed us all in a direct stare. His black eyes didn't miss a thing. Abuelito stood in the middle of the living room. He spoke in short, clipped words and phrases.

"Anna Mae and Malcolm Botts, my grandson Raul." Abuelito pointed as he named each one of us.

"Raul, Malcolm, and Anna Mae went on a treasure hunt for Jefferson Davis' lost Confederate gold for a school project."

Mr. Armando didn't blink. The chair plopped down on all four legs. He leaned forward. He kept his eyes directed at Abuelito. "They require a safe place to hide the gold bags they found until the legality of this mess is straightened out through the proper channels."

No reaction from Mr. Armando. His lips remained shut. I felt like a bug being examined under a microscope. I didn't like the way his face looked. His lips didn't curve up or down. I hardly saw his chest rise and fall. He didn't make a sound, not even a burp or a fart. Was he for real? I felt like I was a criminal under suspicion for theft. Was that the word I wanted? Several others passed through my mind. He laced his fingers together and chewed on something that was stored in his bulging cheek.

"Can you help us?" Abuelito turned his back and walked to the couch where Abuelita and Granma sat. I perched on the edge of the couch. Raul stood behind the couch with Malcolm. They both leaned against it. I knew this for a fact because the couch kept inching forwards.

I expected Mr. Armando to answer in a deep voice. Was I surprised when he replied in a thin, high voice! "Of course, Miguel. that's what friends are for. I've just the place. Let me give you a receipt—standard office policy."

Abuelito smiled. They shook hands. "Need help in getting those bags into the armored vehicle?" Abuelito asked.

Secret Agent Man Mr. Armando shook his head. "I brought my son, Gil, with me. He can help load it. He's a runningback for the University of Georgia's football team this year. Strong enough, I dare say."

Granma led the way out of the living room. Mr. Armando got up from the chair and followed her out into the hallway. I tagged along behind them. At the front door he turned and said to Abuelito, "Nice hearing from you. It's been too long. Jefferson Davis' gold..." He shook his head as Granma opened the front door. "Keep the door locked. No sense in getting careless. I'll phone you tomorrow. Night, folks."

He left the house. I ran to the living room picture window and looked out. Mr. Armando walked in large strides to the armored car. He opened the door and climbed up into the cab. Mr. Armando backed the armored car into our driveway. I ran from the living room, through the dining room, into the kitchen, and darted through the connecting door to the garage. That door was still open.

His kid, Gil, stepped down from the armored car. He was dressed in an old football jersey and black jeans. He, too, wore pointed cowboy boots. Gil walked up to the station wagon and opened the rear door. He reached in. I saw him carry the first bag out and up to the rear end of the armored truck.

Mr. Armando had opened the rear doors of the truck. He stood at its side, and watched as Gil did all the work.

Ten minutes later all the bags were stored in the armored truck. Gil shut the wagon's rear door. He walked back and joined his father. Together, they closed the massive double black doors. Mr. Armando bolted and locked them, then he pocketed the key.

Before leaving, Secret Agent Man turned and waved. I raised my hand and waved back. Emptied of emotion, I walked back to the house. I heard the truck's engine roar. Mr. Armando must've gunned it. They drove off into the unknown.

The excitement over for the day, I closed the garage door and locked it. Granma was in the kitchen, washing the supper dishes. She stopped. Her hands floated on the soapy surface. "Don' fret, chile. Miguel knows wha' he's doin'. He and Juanita are in the livin' room with the boys. Ask 'em t' come out t' the kitchen."

I shuffled out of the kitchen, entered the dining room and walked into the living room. Raul and Malcolm were playing video games on the television screen. It looked like Roach Woman. I saw Abuelita's head resting against her husband's chest. Abuelito lifted his head. His eyes were full of questions marks.

"Granma wan's t' speak with yo'."

Abuelita lifted her head. Abuelito stood up. "I'll be back soon, then we'll leave. Anna Mae, please stay with her. Raul, Malcolm, come with me, please."

I disobeyed and followed them into the kitchen. Granma had finished the dishes. She sat down at the table. Her hands were clasped in front of her. I squeezed in behind the boys. Neither Malcolm nor Raul even noticed that I was there. Everyone looked at Granma Zora. She sagged before our eyes. Miguel walked up to her and placed his arm around her shoulders.

"Zora, is there anything else that I can do for you before we leave?"

Her face changed. Her eyes filled with tears. She reached for a napkin and blew her nose.

"Wha' 'bout Anna Mae and tha' fire at school? I know she didn' start it. We both know how the police work. Minorities are treated different from Caucasians. I know tha' 'less Anna Mae is cleared of arson she'll be charged by the police. Wha' can I do?"

Abuelito sighed. He locked eyes with Granma. "I've been thinking about what Raul told us when he came home from school yesterday. He spends a lot of time watching "Forensic Detective" on television—when we let him. He tells me there are certain types of laboratory tests that can be done to find substances on clothing."

"I have another close acquaintance that was in charge of the military police. I believe he's still involved in that line of work."

"The FBI?" Raul asked, "Abuelito, you never told me!"

"May I use your phone again? It's a Friday night. I think he might still be at the office." All eyes fastened on Abuelito as he picked up the kitchen phone. He punched in the numbers. It seemed to take forever. At last Abuelito spoke into the phone.

"Good evening, Charles." Abuelito nodded his head up and down. "It's been awhile. You got a minute? I need a favor."

Abuelito turned his face away from us. I heard him say, "Someone had to do it...I was there...I didn't stop to think. I threw the damn thing. I'm respectable now. Got a grandson to raise. Yes, never heard. Can you do a test to determine if a person vomited on their clothing? I'll have the clothes ready for you. Tomorrow morning? See you then. Thanks!"

Abuelito put the phone back into its cradle. "He agrees with Raul. There is a test. He'll pick up Malcolm's and Anna Mae's soiled clothing tomorrow morning at our house."

Once I heard that, I flew out of the kitchen, stormed into the shed and sped into the bathroom. I flung the hamper cover up and dug out our clothes   Upstairs, I heard Malcolm stomping up in his room. I shrugged my shoulders and kept heaping the clothes on the floor.

I rushed back into the kitchen and dropped the clothing on the table. Granma handed me a green garbage bag. I tossed the clothing into it.

"Where's Malcolm?"

"Upstairs," Raul said.

Feet hammered on the steps. Malcolm ran into the kitchen, out of breath, and dropped his clothes into the bag when I held it open for him. Granma held out her arms. Malcolm dashed into them. She pulled him to her chest and hugged him.

I held the bag out to Abuelito. He took it from me and tied it off with a rubber band.

"I'll let you know what Charles has to say. The test takes twenty-four hours. Expect a call from me on Monday night. The lab's closed during the weekends. Raul, are you ready?"

"What about my wet clothing?"

"I'm sure Anna Mae will be seeing us soon. Say your good-byes, and then let's go," Abuelito said.

"The Protectora works in mysterious ways," Abuelita said. She hugged me, kissed Granma on the cheek and tried hugging Malcolm. He squirmed out of her tight embrace.

Granma smiled, stood up, and led them into the hallway. I stayed behind. I thought I heard someone whisper behind me. Turning, I glanced into the darkened hallway that led into the shed, but I saw nothing. I fled out of the kitchen and watched as Raul, Aubuelita, and Abuelito left. Granma shut the door behind them and sagged against it.

"We had quite a day, didn't we?" Granma asked me.

"I guess."

Malcolm started singing off key, "We're rich! We're rich!" Stomping his feet and waving his arms, Malcolm danced up the stairs. I heard him as he reached the second floor and continued singing at the top of his lungs. Granma stretched her arms out and snagged me. She pulled me in and hugged me. "Yo' nevah t'old for a hug, Anna Mae. Nevah, don' forget."

Chapter Twenty-three

At 7 p.m. Monday evening the phone rang. Granma picked it up on the second ring. She nodded. "Go on with yo'. Yo' don' say? Merciful heavens!"

I leaned my head close to the receiver, hoping to catch a stray word or two. Granma pushed me away. I retreated to the kitchen table and drummed my fingernails on its surface. She finally finished the conversation and placed the phone in its cradle.

"That was Miguel." I held my breath. "He gave Charles the garbage bag. Charles took it t' the forensic lab. Both yo' and Malcolm's clothes were checked with some kind of light. Charles called Miquel and told him tha' the lab found vomit on ya'll's clothes, both Malcolm's pants and yo' tee shirt.

"Charles thinks when Malcolm vomited some of it spattered on 'em. They found traces on his shirt and on yo' skirt. I guess Malcolm must've left some residue when yo' took the notebook papah from him and put it in yo' pocket, Anna Mae.

"One othahh thin'—Armando sent his son Gil ovah t' the main road tha' y'all walk t' get t' school. He found somethin' of yo's."

I shook. A sudden chill swept over me. "Y-y-y-yes?"

"Gil found a gingah root lyin' in the middle of the street." Granma fixed me with a look that seared right through me. She continued. "Miguel tells me tha' Gil brought tha' root home with 'em and showed it t' his daddy. Armando contacted Charles and told 'em 'bout it.

"Charles stopped by Mistah Armando's home and picked up the root. He took the lab report, gingah root, and y'all's clothin' t' the police and fire marshall. Charles believed tha' they would listen t' reason comin' from a federal agen'. Yo' now cleared of startin the fire. Oh, an' one othahh thin'. Miguel told me t' tell yo' be careful with yo' conjurin'. People may not like it much." She looked down at her hands. "People are still fightin' the war here. Best yo' 'member tha'."

"I hope the police and the fire marshall are happy now tha' they've got their proof."

"It's yo' word 'gainst Pit Bull's; he's an adventurer. It seems tha' Charles believes y'all wild goose story 'bout Jefferson Davis' gold. He's on y'all's side. Count yo' blessin's. It could've been worse.

"The school nurse spoke with Principal Teddy. She told 'em tha' Malcolm made a pit stop tha' mornin', complainin' of chills. Wha' really saved y'all's skins was tha' the fire marshall thinks tha' the fire started aftah yo' and Malcolm sashayed int' school. When the sheriff heard tha' he put some pressure on Lola t' see if she would stick t' her story. She didn'."

"And Stanley Paxton's daddy? Who does he believe? Me or Pit Bull? I'm not bankin' on it bein' me, tha's for sure."

"Funny thin'. It seems tha' Stanley Paxton's daddy had a sit-down talk with his son. Nevah did tha' 'fore. Miguel says tha' Stanley broke down and told the truth for a change. First thin' he said was tha' he poured siphoned gasoline from a lawn mowah they had found stored in the basement on the papers, and placed 'em in the basement's air vents. Lola struck a match and threw it in."

"I wouldn' have thought of doin' tha' in a zillion years," I said.

"Do tell. Yo' got a lot more sense than tha', chile. The othahh news is tha' school starts next Monday mornin'. Portable classrooms are bein' set up. A class schedule will be delivered t' all of the students' parents as t' wha' time their children should report."

I sighed. "Anythin' else I should know 'bout?"

"Yes. It seems tha' Pit Bull wanted t' get even for yo' seein' 'em cry. Tha's why he set the fire and blamed yo' and Malcolm. It was an adventurer's word against a newcomah. Wha' did yo' do?"

"Raul, Malcolm, and I weren' the only kids tha' saw the floating black fist. When Raul and Malcolm left, Pit Bull turned up. He threw a spitball at me. I guess the black fist dinna like tha', cuz it suddenly grew largah and largah and blocked Stanley from walkin' int' the buildin'. Stanley freaked and fell on the ground. He blubbahed. Didn't I tell you?"

Granma shook her head and laughed. "Don' 'member yo' tellin' me tha. It must've slipped my mind. Enjoy the rest of the week. Next Monday is yo' first day of school 'gain. 'Fore I forget, Miguel did say two othahh thin's. He tole me tha' the hero always gets the girl at the end of the case." She paused.

"Wha's the second thin'?"

"Look int' yo' room and receive the blessin' of yo' Protectora."

"There's nothin' in my room, 'cept the bed, dressah, closet..."

Granma fixed her eyes on me. "Are yo' sure? Maybe, yo' bettah check it 'gain."

"I will," I said. "I wondah why he said tha'." Granma smiled her Cheshire cat smile, serene and mysterious.

"Don' yo' know? Raul tole 'em t' tell yo' tha' yo' were *his gal.*"

I covered my face with my hands "G-r-a-n-m-a!"

"I tole yo', Raul's in love with yo'."

She walked out of the kitchen, grinning that famous smile of hers. I stared at the floor. A gooey warmth spread over me like a protective blanket. Raul, in love with me. Who would've guessed it?

Above me, someone laughed. I looked up at the ceiling. The disembodied black fist appeared first. His wedding ring glinted in the florescent light. The rest of his body appeared in sections.

First came his straw hat. It fit tight on his cropped black hair. I guessed that he must've stood about 5 foot 10 inches tall. He had brown eyes set deep in an oval face. His smile was tight-lipped. A coarse, gray-specked white beard fell from his chin. I couldn't help myself. I stared. My mouth dropped open. He wore a Confederate uniform—a grey tattered jacket and faded blue cast-off pants. They covered his upper thighs. Caked dirt clothed the remainder of his bare legs. His black high boots reached to his knees. His toes stuck through three large holes in his socks. I gagged. He smelled of vomit, body odor, and coffee. It near knocked me over. I wanted to run out of the kitchen, but I stayed.

I noticed that he wore several leather straps around his neck. All kinds of stuff hung off of the straps: a dented canteen, two tin cups, and a loose-burlap sack shaped like Momma's over-the-shoulder-boulder-holder-bag.

"Wha' are yo' starin' at, chile? Haven' yo' evah seen a soldah of the Lord?"

"N-n-n-n-o," I said.

He brought up one of his arms. "Here. I wuz tol' t' give yo' this. 'From a friend,' she says." The soldier dropped a three-legged silver bowl in front of me. Rose and lavender petals fell to the floor, twirling and circling the bowl as it floated to the linoleum. I inhaled their sweet fragrance. My mind cleared. Then I saw it. A scrap of paper fell from the silver bowl.

I stooped and picked it up.

"*Next!*"

✦ THE END ✦

Picture of Confederate Soldier
from the Smithsonian

Free Black Men Fought on the Confederate Side

Towards the end of The War Between the States, the Union Army started using blacks in combat situations. Many of these units were commanded by white officers. These blacks were kept apart from the white units and treated with disdain and contempt until the officers realized that black soldiers made excellent fighters. They could attack and triumph a superior white force of armed white men.

Unknown to many, the Confederates started accepting free black men to fight in the Southern ranks. They either bought their freedom from their southern masters or they were from Haiti, Jamaica, or other Caribbean Islands and were plantation owners themselves. These blacks, like their white brethren, felt threatened by loss of economic revenue and way of life.

In *The Anna Mae Mysteries: The Golden Treasure*, mention of a phantom black soldier appears throughout the story. This particular free black soldier lived and served on the Confederate side as a Sergeant First Class.

Spanish Everyone?

Abuelita – grandmother

Abuelito – grandfather

Gracias, Señor – Thank you, Mister.

Gracias, Señorita – Thank you, Miss.

Numbers – Counting to ten

Uno	One
Dos	Two
Tress	Three
Cuatro	Four
Cinco	Five
Seis	Six
Siete	Seven
Ocho	Eight
Nueve	Nine
Diez.	Ten

Bibliography/Resources

Andrews, Ted. *Psychic Power* (Dragonhawk Publishing, Jackson, Tennessee, 2000)

Chennault Plantation – Legends of Lost Gold – An online Article:
http://www.kudcom.com/chennault/gold.html

Classic South of Georgia, Washington – An online Article:
http://www.comeandenjoygeorgia.com/classic%20south_georgia.htm

González-Wippler, Migene, *Santería: The Religion* (Llewellyn Publications, St. Paul, Minnesota, 2004)

Horton, Amy, The Lore of Rebel Gold – An online Article:
http://www.rootsweb.com/~gabrantl/confedgold2.htm

Lenz, Richard J. The Civil War in Georgia, An Illustrated Travelers Guide – The Mystery of the Confederate Treasure – An online Article:
http://sherpaguides.com/georgia/civil_war/sidebars/mystery_of_the_confederate_treasure

Preserve America Community: Washington, Georgia – An online Article:
http://www.prserveamerica.gov/PAcommunity-washingGA.html

Thompson, Sr., Scott R. The Day the President Came to Town – An online Article:
http://organizations.nlamerica.com/hardy/MilitaryHistory/day_the_president_came_to_town

Washington, Georgia – Lost Confederate Gold – Legend of the Lost Gold of the Confederacy – An Online Article:
http://www.kudcom./www/gold.html

Waynesville, Brantley County, Georgia, What Ever Happened To The Confederate Gold? "The Question of Confederate Gold" – Two Online Articles:
http://www.rootsweb.com/~gabrantl/confedgold.html

Additional References to Santeria and the Orishas – Excerpted from online resource:
http://www.balus-den.com/pataki.htm

Feedback

Did you enjoy reading the first book in the series: The Anna Mae Mysteries: The Golden Treasure? Email your comments to me at lillian@authorsden.com.

Look for the second book in The AM Mysteries. The Anna Mae Mysteries: King Solomon's Ark.

Three 'tween sneaker sleuths search for King Solomon's Ark while being chased by a dethroned African Emperor and his sons.

Questions

- Why did the South call the Civil War the War Between the States?

- Who were the Blacks who fought on the side of the Confederacy?

- Who borrowed the gold from the French?

- How much was the gold worth during The War Between the States?

- How many ghost soldiers approach Anna Mae and for who did they fight?

- Where is Chennault Plantation located?

- Why doesn't Anna Mae trust the Georgia police?

- Where does Granma Zora live during the summer?

- How was Jefferson Davis captured at the end of the war?

- Why did Pit Bull and Lola Simms hate Anna Mae?

- What started the school fire?

- What grade was Raul and Anna Mae in?

- How do you feel about the children being treated differently?

- What would you do?

Email your answers to lillian@authorsden.com.

All replies will be posted on The Anna Mae Mysteries site and will be discussed in the forum, blog, Anna Mae's newsletter, and chatroom.